KIND MIRRORS,
UGLY GHOSTS

Published in the United States by:
Archway Editions
a division of powerHouse Cultural Entertainment, Inc.
32 Adams Street, Brooklyn, NY 11201

www.archwayeditions.us

Daniel Power, CEO
Chris Molnar, Founder and Editorial Director
Nicodemus Nicoludis, Founder and Managing Editor
Naomi Falk, Senior Editor

Edited by Naomi Falk
Proofread by José Carpio

Library of Congress Control Number: 2020950785

ISBN 978-1-64823-039-4

Printed by Toppan Leefung

First edition, 2023

10 9 8 7 6 5 4 3 2 1

Cover image © the Jimmy DeSana Trust. Courtesy of the Jimmy DeSana Trust
and P·P·O·W, New York

Printed and bound in China

ARCHWAY
EDITIONS

KIND MIRRORS, UGLY GHOSTS

CLAIRE DONATO

Archway Editions, Brooklyn, NY

CONTENTS

Last night, she dreamt she was a ghost. She was walking on her street and couldn't find her home. Then she awoke in the world to drink a mug filled with lukewarm water and the juice of one lemon. She does not feel the same [*she takes a sip*], nor does she feel undead [*she takes another*]. Rather, she experiences this daily ritual as a minute change from one color (streetlights and vintage gas lamps illuminating houses) to the next (a series of successive changes meant to set the stage for stepping away from life's plateau). In the midst, she floats on her back in acidic water [*watching the wind rip the leaves off the trees*], defying death. It is a bright summer's day. She is not yet awake. The sky—a reflective surface within whose upper and lower portions she is refracted—is scattered in all directions. As she takes the last sip [*amen*], there is a period of inertia: . Then the graceless caesura arrives near the end of the line, indicating a pause—||—yet it's too late to share breath. The story is over. Nothing is left.

COLOUR GREEN

Why are you asking me to write a story?

> *Is it processing?*
> *No.*
> *Is it fantasy?*
> *No.*
> *Is it therapy?*
> *No.*

/

Spring is green, and a succulent plant is green, and an unread message is green, and *Colour Green* is the name of a record a woman sends to a stranger on the second night of their correspondence. This correspondence takes place on Christmas Eve in four-dimensional reality—via an electronic messaging system—where there always exists the possibility one may fall, befall. In writing, she expresses her thoughts freely, and is honest. In three-dimensional reality—"real life"—it is difficult for her to speak, trapped as she is between French—her first language—and English. When she does speak, her truest perceptions of the world feel impossible to articulate, nor can she obfuscate them with a story. And so she remains caught between silence and truth. "Truth is always an interior and inexplicable contact," wrote the dead experimental novelist Clarice Lispector, whose name contains her own: *Claire*, a second name meaning *clear, bright, pure, transparent, famous.* But Clarice Lispector did not even write in English. Clarice Lispector spoke Portuguese; Clarice Lispector wrote in Portuguese. And Claire does not speak; she does not write stories. And so too is Claire's reflection unclear.

With the stranger, Claire shares her desire to write a story in which a narrator named No falls in love with a plant. The plant is a succulent, but for the purpose of the story, it is also important that the word *plant* invokes a person posing as someone they are not, a spy or some sort of informant placed into a zone that is not theirs for nefarious reasons.

Over the span of six years, Claire explains, she has written several drafts of the story of No and the plant, which has never been called "Colour Green." Rather, the story is called "Noëlle," after her narrator's full name, meaning *Christmas*. In one version of "Noëlle," No, who lives in Los Angeles, meets the plant via a hookup website on December 25th, messages with it, and picks it up in a health food store parking lot in Echo Park. In another version, No drives to the Santa Monica Pier with the plant seated next to her, but before they reach their destination, the story devolves into an elaborate description of *Colour Green,* an early 1970s folk record by German singer-songwriter Sibylle Baier. In a third version of "Noëlle," the plant is seated across from No in her living room, which is adorned with icicle lights and fresh flowers. Together, the two protagonists stay awake (the plant may be a plant; it may also be a person who is a plant) until 2:00 a.m., listening to *Colour Green.* "I want to tell you everything" is something No says aloud to the plant in this iteration of the story, and Claire recognizes this dialogue as poorly constructed, trite. Her reader, she fears, will feel nothing. He will deem her a hack; he will abandon hers for another story; or he will read a novel—one that progresses along a continuum of linear time and does not fall victim to its author's digressions and sexual fantasies.

In her correspondence with the stranger, Claire describes *Colour Green*—not the story, but the aforementioned early 1970s folk record by German singer-songwriter Sibylle Baier. From memory, Claire details its backstory to the plant via text message. At age sixteen,

Baier took a trip to Strasbourg and the Alps in Genoa with her friend Claudine. Baier was in a period of depression, and Claudine wanted to cheer her up—so the story goes. When Baier returned to Germany, she wrote and recorded her first song, "Remember the Day," a one-minute and forty-four-second reflection on her trip, her suicidal thoughts before it, and the feeling of aliveness she experienced in Genoa. "Remember that day / When I left home to buy some food / Considering if one shouldn't die or if one should," Baier sings. "I found me on the road to Genoa."

baier sings in a low register, Claire messages the stranger. *like honey, her songs are slow and sepia-toned <3*

the song goes on, Claire types, and she pastes more lyrics into her message:

> *There slowly, slowly, I no longer thought of what is good or what is not*
> *There simply was the water's smell and remoteness*
> *I only stood and watched that old, cold ocean*
> *In tender and bright, full, unspeakable emotion*
> *I did what I could*
> *All was good*

The stranger does not respond. This may be because his phone is on silent; because he is not at his phone; because he lost his phone; because his phone's system automatically updated and is no longer compatible with hers; because he is shy; because he is strong and silent; because he is angry; because he is a man who delivers bread-crumbs, small morsels of interest meant to lead her on; because he is only interested in sexting; or because he is not an animate being.

Because of her experience in psychoanalysis, and because she yearns for intimacy while desiring to remain alone, Claire chooses to perceive the man's silence as listening, and therefore continues messaging him.

i like the lyric "i no longer thought of what is good or what is not," Claire says. *it's a reminder we can free ourselves from moral strictures, but then the song plays a trick on us and recursively loops back to the moral category of "good" anyway :)*

After composing "Remember the Day," Sibylle Baier continued writing and recording songs on a reel-to-reel tape machine in her home over the course of three years. She distributed a few copies, the story once again goes, although it is sometimes also purported she shared the music with no one, that the record was never intended for public consumption. Ultimately, Baier stored the master tapes in her attic for thirty years until one Christmas, her son discovered them, and burnt *Colour Green* onto multiple CDs, and gave these CDs away to family members, and to a famous musician instrumental in reissuing the record, which now plays in millennial bars and mumblecore movies.

"How can a sixteen-year-old sound so grown up and cosmopolitan?" one music critic asks. "And how can Baier—a German native—sing in such flawless English?"

To the stranger, Claire writes: *i've connected with everyone i've ever loved (lol) thanks to this record.* She often accentuates her more serious sentences with emoticon smiley faces, hearts, and electronic laughter, forms of punctuation meant to set the stranger at ease, and to please him.

e.g, i once bought the record for a vegan who, despite his constrained diet, was addicted to pornography and central nervous system depressants. he was obsessed with the song "i lost something in the hills" and i think wound up recording a cover of it

"i grew up in declivities / others grow in cities" is a lyric from that song. Claire pauses and copy and pastes a link to the song, which appears as a hyperlinked image in its own message:

https://www.youtube.com/watch?v=N-oERBst8Lo

i was 12 and in the middle of 7th grade when my mom and i moved to a town in western pa whose thickly wooded forests felt like downward slopes. my mom, a french immigrant, was suddenly a single mother finishing her dissertation while working as an adjunct professor, so the move was tough. we lived in a chintzy modular apartment building next door to a wendy's and a kfc. after school i'd buy spicy chicken sandwiches and frosties and listen to music and scratch into my room's walls with my nails. the walls were white and paper thin and made of plaster—easy to dig into. the hollows i carved were depressions :(

the town, Claire adds, *was called clarion. like my name!*

this song, "i lost something in the hills," reminds me that i'm unsure whether growing up in a town evocative of my name caused me to become trapped at the bottom of a declivity that no amount of talking can cure. does this make sense?

The plant does not respond, which establishes a sense of urgency and longing. Giving and giving to the plant, Claire observes, feels like a form of creation.

based on the story of sibylle baier's son finding and sharing colour green with j mascis—Claire names the musician who passed along *Colour Green* to Orange Twin, the record's label—*i like to imagine that sb came from a 'good' family—i.e. a family whose constellation of members—mother, father, daughter, son, &c.—stick together, and whose so-called resilience western society deems to be virtuous*

but sometimes it feels like the nuclear family is doomed

do you think the demands placed upon it are existentially impossible?

my teenage years in clarion symbolized that impossibility

if sibylle baier had immigrated to america like my mom, she would've thrown away those leftover copies of colour green and no one would've ever heard her music

anyway, you might also appreciate that sb once appeared in a wim wenders movie :)

sorry!!

xo, Claire signs off, indicating flirtation.

In the third draft of the story Claire wants to write, Noëlle AKA No sits in her living room across from the plant with whom she wants to share everything and plays "Tonight" from *Colour Green* on loop. No watches as the plant listens and becomes greener and fantasizes about extending her fingers outward toward its leaves. After studying the plant for some time, she, like a cat, takes a bite. The plant oozes green liquid that tastes a lot like cilantro. No bites down again, then slowly licks the plant's juices, running her tongue along its leaves, then sucks each leaf like a key lime popsicle. The plant does not make a sound, nor does it bite back—it is silent—so the dynamic continues this way for some time: No gnawing and sucking on the plant's leaves, licking, and then swallowing its fluids. Subsequently, No and the plant listen to "Forget About," and "Softly," and "Says Elliott," and "I Lost Something in the Hills" from *Colour Green* until dawn arrives and there are no more leaves left.

Claire messages a .zip file containing all of the tracks from *Colour Green* to the four-dimensional stranger who is also a plant, a spy. He says he fixed his phone after he dropped and cracked it while putting it in a drawer. He stows it away to ensure that he is not distracted while working. Claire considers whether this is a lie, like when he claims he is interested not only in the lost female singer-songwriters of the late 1970s, but also in consensual sadomasochistic practices as they might manifest on the Internet. She suspects that he is only interested in the latter, though she likes the way he pretends to be a fan of Sibylle Baier: *I'm listening now and it's lovely,* he messages. *Do you want one partner for kinky sex and one for romance?*

i want a kinky partner, and i want a romantic partner, Claire says, *but i can't seem to find either*

Where have you looked?

not much of anywhere. websites. i'm anxious because of my job. like what if my students see me?

You don't need to put your face on those websites.

i don't ;) are you still listening to sibylle baier?

You're part of a secret sex society that exists in plain sight, the stranger says. *Living a double life is part of the gambit. You'll get used to it.*

In a series of messages to the plant, Claire describes her sexual proclivities.

i like to be hit and i like to be cut, she explains. *i like dark bruises, although i don't like to be hit across my face*

do you like to be hit, or do you like to do the hitting? i have a lot of profiles throughout a range of dating and hookup websites, but my interests on them are boring. and though i like talking about sex, the physical act of it makes me feel sick. according to freud, i'm a hysteric :)

love *feels* like something i *should* desire, but i *want* to be alone. which is probably something i should analyze?

when i'm hit during sex, i feel my consciousness float away from my body until it attaches itself to the ceiling and watches me being beaten

re: slow dancing: that sort of closeness feels like the scene in twin peaks where leland slow dances with maddie until he kills her. in love, i guess i'm always slow dancing with a projection of my father before being smashed into a framed poster of missoula, montana

Although Claire decided that the plant must have put his phone in a drawer so he could work, she copies an image which she pastes into a message:

have you ever seen this photograph by francesca woodman? i identify with both the woman and the turtle, though i spend more time gazing at turtles at petco than i do being a woman, so i imagine if i had to be one or the other, i would choose to be the plate

Claire stares at the nothing beyond her phone.

i don't think i know what you look like?

Presently, Claire is sitting on her living room sofa listening to *Colour Green*, fantasizing about where in his body the strange, four-dimensional plant stores pain. She sends the record's eponymous song, "Colour Green," to him. In a message, she pastes a couplet from its lyrics:

Come on and let us try both and take tender care
But when you need help I will be there

The plant does not respond.

i appreciate that you and i can talk about this stuff, Claires messages, then continues writing:

some days i take nude photographs of myself for a scandinavian graphic designer who tells me in great detail about the porn he watches and asks me to look up porn i like and send him screenshots. in exchange, i tell him how i sneak into unstaffed dressing rooms at the gap and steal underwear. i tear the tags off and bunch the underwear into my tote bag, which is labeled armageddon, the place where the last battle between good and evil will be fought

"fall into the gap"—i remembered that jingle while typing

when i logged back into my fetlife account after not logging in for over a year, i had forgotten at one time i was interested in meeting a "vegan sadist," lol. my profile is so earnest!! She logs into her FetLife account (username *forgett*, password *281933!!,* her grandfather's birthday followed by two exclamation points, a comfortable symmetry vis-à-vis *forgett* with two Ts), navigates to her profile, copies its ABOUT section and pastes it into a separate message, then adds quotation marks around it to indicate that the source text is gleaned:

"I am looking to connect with a secure, empathetic, and intelligent vegan or vegetarian dom/switch for a mutually beneficial sexual relationship"

She pauses, then writes:

one of my profile interests is "slaughterhouses (watching)"—like

watching undercover slaughterhouse videos made by vegan activists, with
a vegan sadist. though i don't think i'm into that anymore. are you?
   fucking freakshow!!

To the four-dimensional stranger, Claire professes she has been considering a new occupation, one wherein she receives money in exchange for completing digital tasks such as sending the aforementioned Scandinavian photographs of herself in stolen underwear, narrating fantasies that make him ejaculate, or disclosing specific information about herself including her age, weight, height, and bra size. The plant, who desires to marry an escort, is excited by this prospect. *I can mentor you*, he says. *I have been studying the art of financial domination for years.*

   Within the span of two hours, the plant sends her links to social networking pages where women post half-nude photographs of themselves in juxtaposition with donation links, and creates an account for her on a website where men must deposit money into an account before contacting women. The password for this website is Claire's last name, which the plant tells her she can change. She signs up, change the profile's name to Anastasia, and does nothing.

The plant tells Claire the key to her success in her new occupation rests in the following mantra: *tease, deny, edge, ruin, repeat.* She laughs aloud when she reads this; then the four-dimensional stranger says: *Want to practice?*
   i don't know if I feel like practicing, Claire says.
   LOL, the stranger says.
   but if we were to practice, what would that be like, she says.
   You tell me, he says. *What's your pleasure? Don't be shy.*
   my pleasure is for you to not take your clothes off, she says. *i want you to feel close and very far away*
   How am I doing?

Noëlle aka No is sitting on her bedspread wearing gray and black striped socks. She took a shower and is not wearing makeup, nor has she washed her hair. She is ugly, although the plant wrote to her to say he wants her, and that all women are beautiful. These assertions felt like the truth.

in my fantasy, i take my clothes off, she says to the plant, *but you do not. you are close but also far away, thanks not only to proximity but also to your clothing. this distance protects me*

i ask you to bite your arm, and you bite your arm, she says.

Where, the plant says.

on your left bicep

OK.

i ask you to put your left fingers in your mouth, and you put your left fingers in your mouth

i lick your forearm and remove your fingers from your mouth. you think i'm going to kiss you, but i put my fingers in your mouth instead. they're my left fingers too, so it's as if my hand is yours

This is nice, the plant says.

with my other hand i put your right arm behind your back and clasp your wrist in a firm way

Good.

and then i make you put your left arm around my back so we're pressed together, my fingers still in your mouth, your right arm still behind your back. i tell you to bite and you bite

I like having your fingers in my mouth.

i like putting my fingers in your mouth. i like that i could theoretically yank out your jaw

I like that I could bite off your hand.

what if my sexuality is 85% textual?

Men will pay for it, the plant says.

i'll give it to you for free, she says.
You will?
i just did :) what do you think?
I think you should write a short story.
for you?
No, the plant says. *For you.*

THE ONLY PERSON YOU HURT IS YOURSELF

Upon the recommendation of a friend, I procure a Pentax H3 35mm camera from the 1960s. It is a metal contraption emblazoned with many numbers, most of which I do not understand. Nor do the electronic videos I watch about it effectively instruct me to use it. These videos are primarily crafted by faceless men whose voiceovers attempt to demystify the camera's features. *So there's, uh, a construction variation in the H3—you can see this has a notch in the HT, maybe you can see that? So models made after 1963 have this notch.* Needless to say, I can barely load film into the camera. I ask these men for help. I should have asked a woman.

As I walk with the camera hanging around my neck, I think about writing, about how writing with a camera around one's neck transforms one's relationship to language. I am the "one" in this sentence, or I am one *with* this sentence, but I also use this pronoun—"one"—to cultivate space between myself and the sentence, as the camera cultivates space between myself and the world that is an extension of my sight, insofar as the world is shaped by one's eye while simultaneously remaining separate from it. In the park by the Children's Museum—does this park have a name? ("Words make things name themselves," a poet said)—I chase a squirrel with a nut in its mouth as it moves from the grass to a tree to a ledge where it appears to be racing the course of my gaze, or testing me. As I chase the squirrel, I laugh, then become increasingly self-conscious in relation to the other human beings around me. Do they think I'm trying to take their photograph too? And if they do, what do they think?

I return to my apartment, place the Pentax H3 camera on the mint green desk where I attend video chat psychoanalysis sessions. Prior to the global pandemic, I laid down on a couch next to my analyst and cried and trembled and shook, exorcizing the past. Now I am a trunkless and pixelated analysand who is simultaneously protected and framed by the surface of my life: bookshelves, houseplants, a linen comforter, a framed poster featuring an illustration of a woeful cat. White walls. Even the cure reifies a certain distance. But sometimes a real cat sits on my lap.

When a friend who is staying in my apartment says she is going outside to reunite with her lover, I say I'll stay indoors. It would be strange for me to be downstairs when you greet one another. But I'll look at you both from the window. Not for too long.

Looking out the window, I creep. This is in antithesis to the swift tempo I maintained in the park, chasing the squirrel. At my bedroom window, I feel curious and languorous. Watching my friend embrace her lover makes me physically feel my heart and makes my heart ache. As they hold each other on the sidewalk, time lapses. In front of them, a parked car pulls away; a stone church reflects the sun; an ancient tree grows older. And although I shed nothing, my words become waves.

My friend and her lover drive to the beach. This is five years before they will conceive a child. I stay at home, practice yoga, neglect to read a book. Eventually, I take a second walk with the camera hanging around my neck, and am surprised that I experience an impulse to photograph babies who belong to exhausted-looking parents. Yet I am too shy to ask the exhausted-looking parents if I may photograph their babies. I have no desire to have children but am enamored of photographs of me as a baby and, by extension of this narcissism, desire to photograph other babies whose eyes are very big. My fantasy is that I will take these photographs and mail them to the babies' parents, and in thirty years, the babies will look back upon themselves with a sort of distanced inquisitiveness one might reserve for a Dinosaur Museum or Hall of Gems and Minerals. 2053: Will any of us even be here then?

Back in my apartment, I sift through a plastic container of childhood ephemera and find a photograph of my high school boyfriend as a six-year-old, which he gifted me when we dated. We met when I was fourteen and he was seventeen. He had black hair, and I was overweight. To woo me, he wrote my name in the sand at a beach and took a photograph of it, which I hung in a frame above my bed. Sometimes while I masturbated, I fantasized about us eating french fries, then fucking on the sand. I had not yet lost my virginity, but we held hands in my high school's bleachers, and continued holding hands until he cheated on me with a cheerleader closer to his age, which sounds too on-the-nose to be true, but alas. Probably she was a slut who helped him ejaculate. Which, in retrospect, I wished I was.

I write to my high school boyfriend and ask for his mailing address. Subsequently, I send him his childhood photograph. And thus we begin a brief electronic correspondence about our lives. In this correspondence, my high school boyfriend calls his girlfriend "girlfriend," as if she has no name. She lacks a sense of adventure, he explains, and she spends too much time listening to mental health podcasts, which makes him feel lonely. When he tells me this, I pity her. Maybe pity's not the right word.

In my replies, I tell my high school boyfriend about my hobbies. One of them, I say, is sitting on the floor and doing nothing. I spent a lot of time at a Zen monastery before the year 2020, I say, though I imagine my high school boyfriend has no idea what a Zen monastery is. He works at a craft brewery where a keg of beer recently exploded in his face, knocking out his two front teeth. I imagine the newly punched empty space in his mouth, agape with thirst for beer, and the horsey look of it. He could never be a monk.

It occurs to me that my interest in Zen might be related to my attachment problems. My psychoanalyst once described these issues as "disorganized." This description—*disorganized*—made me feel like an exceptional case, for my apartment is well-maintained and tidy, a structured whole that I fancy to be, per Zen, a reflection of my mind. My psychoanalyst, who is fluent in abandonment discourse and serves as a mirror of sorts (provided I understand the person I see in the mirror isn't really me), narrated with clinical precision the way I get excited to enter a relational container. "Your excitement," she explained, "is always a form of anxiety." When the relational container is achieved, however, I want nothing but to viciously break it. "Thus you sabotage your relationships by cultivating extreme forms of distance between yourself and your partner—one form of distance being the very partner you select," she said. "Both you and your partners want to hurt other people but turn your ire inward. In the end, the only person you hurt is yourself."

As her interpretation of my relational patterns echoed through video, I got very quiet, looked up at the ceiling. All the while, I felt a pair of invisible fists punching my skull's walls. Later, I DMed one book (Italo Calvino's *Six Memos for the Next Millennium*) and two bands (Throbbing Gristle, Suicide) to my high school boyfriend, who I now pictured as a child without his two front teeth, photographed by me in 35mm black and white film. Then I wrote some other sentences to him about why he should try to connect more with his girlfriend, imploring him to try and see things her way, to not fuck this up. I am a writer, so crafting these messages did not feel like extraneous "emotional labor." It was simply my practice. But I did not tell myself this as I gave him my heart.

THE ANALYST

I came to psychoanalysis to mourn the last shards of faith I had in heterosexuality. Into a glass of wine, I say to my ex-partner: I am finally learning to speak. You're saying you never learned to speak, my ex-partner says. Do you know how ridiculous that sounds?

About psychoanalysis, my ex-partner says: It's a dying profession. Why don't you join a support group instead? Al-Anon exists, and I hear there's one where you co-counsel strangers. You take a class and learn to listen to the strangers. You get close with them, I'm told. It's radical, in fact. You go to the strangers once a week for an hour at a time and listen to them, but you can't be friends with or have sex with them. The entire goal of this support group is for people who are strangers to help one another cry.

You can't have sex with your analyst, either. Not that I'd want to.

I suppose you cannot see her, my analyst, so let me paint a picture in your mind. My analyst has emerald green eyes. From the Latin, her name means *industrious, striving.* Physically, she is slender and multi-pronged like the notebook where she writes down my thoughts as she listens, after which she offers observations: incantations that invoke supernatural forms, hidden places, and the dead. Hovering in attention, her eyes remain fixed in a look one might refer to as *meditative.* Underneath them exists an abyss where light becomes trapped, where she too is trapped inside. *I feel formless today*, I imagine her thinking, and one might claim I am projecting, trivializing her mood as nothing more than a sentence in her head. And perhaps I don't understand her, but I insist I know her: her chapped lips; her tortoiseshell glasses; her dislike of cold; and her ability to win strangers over with a self-deprecating sense of humor, a quality absent in most human beings. While speaking, she pauses to consider the mood of each phrase. With so many words at one's disposal, one must carefully choose.

My analyst: she is me, as I am her. We have already begun to tell our story.

On days we are dressed in all black, I imagine I am her—my analyst, my kind mirror—and she is me—an austere adjunct, an ugly ghost, a writer's writer who got her heart smashed to bits by the last heterosexual man she'll ever love: a long-distance inamorata who, before pausing to kiss her goodbye, said: *We should just be friends.*

Because she knows what secure attachment is, my analyst feels sorry for me. She does not say so, but I see it, gazing at her through my peripheral vision as I lie face-up on the couch. I dreamt I was forced to perform oral sex on a dead dick, I say. I am in love with a body that is not a body, I say. I came home, made an açai bowl, wept on my cat, and emailed you, I say. Our correspondence helps me write.

What does my analyst think of my porousness? You are going to write a book, I tell her. It will be called *Kind Mirrors, Ugly Ghosts*. It will be about a psychoanalyst who is trying to write a novel when she is supposed to be writing a monograph. *Kind Mirrors, Ugly Ghosts* will experimentally juxtapose excerpts from the monograph-in-progress—a series of case studies about world-weary analysands whose psychic woes induce negative counter-transference in the analyst, haunting emotions she cannot exorcise, no matter how many smudge sticks she burns—with a wry inner monologue that elucidates how, while writing her monograph, the analyst chain smokes, eats jelly beans, and becomes distracted by online news articles about North American orca populations starving and disappearing. The novel will contain a ten-page passage about how the analyst is preparing for life after Roe v. Wade; a flashback to an afternoon she served as a hospice volunteer; a chapter called "Enema"; erasures of pages from Freud's *The Joke and Its Relation to the Unconscious*; and drafts of emails she sends to her monograph's academic publisher, wherein she concocts a fiction detailing a recently developed water allergy that is causing her to fall behind deadline. Ultimately, the juxtaposition between the monologue and the monograph will produce the novel's alchemy, described by *The New York Times Book Review* as "neurotically rhizomatic."

I will write a novel too. My novel will be about you. It will be called *The Analyst*, and it will take place inside the mind of an unreliable narrator who is obsessed with her psychoanalyst. The novel will be an homage to *Lolita*: delusional and tongue-in-cheek, but with less blatant erotic motifs. I want my prose to feel like Nabokov, but a little more repressed. Writing is the drive to live, but sentences inevitably lead toward death. This morning, I wrote a list in my phone, and the list may be an outline for the novel, or it may be the novel itself. Novels can assume a number of forms, I explain. I learned this in graduate school. After all, the novel is about making literature novel. These days, the novel is not necessarily a paper object; it is a container, a malleable form with malleable boundaries for this malleable century in which the world is a grief that creeps up the spine and pauses in the center, shadowing the heart. In other words, Extended JavaScript can be a novel. Sans serif phrases projected atop buildings, per Jenny Holzer—expiring for love is beautiful but stupid; all I am is impulse, and longing; and only by enough, to contemplate from afar—can be a novel. A bowl filled with chopped vegetables and ink on paper can be a novel—and a balloon filled with scraps of language, a cross-stitched text, a deck of cards, and so forth.

Balloons make me depressed, my analyst says. They lay dead on the beach like whale carcasses.

I fantasize about going on a writing retreat with my analyst, my kind mirror, my sister, my best friend. In psychoanalysis, fantasy is sometimes spelled *phantasy*, and refers to a situation imagined by an analysand wherein certain desires are revealed. Phantasies may not be real, but they may be *realistic*. They can be sexual in nature, but mine are not. Rather, in my phantasy, my analyst and I meet when I am 30. She is 36—an age that makes her feel more like a sister than an older friend—and we bond over our bleak views of romantic love, shared affinity for Arthur Russell, and the scene in the new *Twin Peaks* where Laura Palmer screams in the Red Room. When I arrive at a coffee shop holding a bouquet of flowers in my arms, my analyst laughs and says: *Dead, wrapped in plastic.* A barista smiles. The amount of energy created when my analyst and I are together is magnetic! Together, our purpose is to bring something extraordinary to the world that betters the planet. Both of us are committed to zero waste in our homes; both of us are currently reading Naomi Klein's *This Changes Everything: Capitalism vs. The Climate;* both of us know the farmers from whom we purchase heirloom blue eggs; both of us own insulated stainless steel coffee mugs for hot coffee and tea; both of us are members of the Woodstock Farm Sanctuary; and both of us use facial toner made from apple cider vinegar, witch hazel extract, and filtered water. How we meet is not part of my phantasy—it is as if we fell out of the sky and into each other's lives—but because we both live in Brooklyn, the majority of our bonding takes place in Prospect Park. There, we circle the lake and comment upon men—"that one looks safe; that one looks like he rapes"—and talk about the loneliness of being only children while laughing at ducks I photograph and send to my mother, an avid collector of all things related to waterfowl. My mother collects rubber ducks too, my analyst says, and it is in this moment I know we are friends.

In Park Slope, my analyst and I rent a car at a car rental agency where I once rented a car with my ex-partner. Before renting the car, we purchase macrobiotic sushi and mango kombucha at the Park Slope Food Coop, where we work together once a month for two hours and forty-five minutes, and where today we overheard a mother tell her child about a friend who had a hysterectomy accompanied by marital woes in great detail. *Let's share sad stories*, the mother said to the child, who subsequently pretended to choke herself.

When I work checkout shifts at the food coop, I scan strangers' groceries. As I scan their groceries, the strangers and I discuss our lives. Do you write poetry, I ask a stranger I've never met. No, I'm training to be a psychoanalyst, she says. How funny, I say. I want to be a psychoanalyst too. This winter, I plan to enroll in a class on Oedipal complexes. As the phrase slips from my tongue—Oedipal complexes—I note my use of the verb *to be enrolled*, as if psychoanalysis is a school, and I, its student. It is so expensive, after all. It is putting me in debt.

Yes, but is it making you feel good?

I begin to recite a list of psychoanalytic texts I've recently ingested: books by Lou Andreas-Salomé, Jamieson Webster, Serge Leclaire, Julia Kristeva—and Lacan, whose first name I can never remember. The stranger types these names into her cell phone. It was good to listen to you, she says.

The stranger's eyes contain a glimmer of recognition I have been noticing in other people as of late. The people whose eyes contain this glimmer are also enrolled in psychoanalysis. I know this because I am open: I am not ashamed to be psychoanalysis's student, and as such, I make my enrollment known. I am in psychoanalysis four days a week, I say, drinking wine at a literary event. *Just leaving analysis, meet you in ten,* I type to a colleague. *Couldn't stop making a frenetic, orb-like gesture with my hands in analysis whilst deploying the verb "to cathect,"* I declare to the Internet, the great void.

My disclosures do not mean I lack boundaries. Quite the opposite. They are declarations indicating how my boundaries are so set they are, in fact, open—so radically open: open to the world and to possibility, to self-exploration and a deeper sense of the abyss. I am open to freely speaking, and to resisting the experience of feeling shame around my most vulnerable attributes. Genetic disgrace is not my fault: I was raised Catholic; I was raised to feel guilty. Psychoanalysis is the box where I place my darkest thoughts and transgressions, where I absolve myself of sin. In this way, it is more like confession than school, but because I attended Catholic school, confession was part of my academic curriculum. In other words, I have completed the necessary prerequisites for and possess inner depth associated with the psychoanalytic model.

In our rental car, my analyst and I drive to a nearby beach town somewhere in the Hamptons, a stretch of land to which I've never been, to which I'll never go. I'm not sure how we can afford to be here, I say to my analyst. You are a freelancer, and I am an adjunct. Nevertheless, we are subletting a sun-soaked, minimalist three-story home whose floor-to-ceiling glass windows look out upon the ocean, whose kitchen's stainless steel appliances gleam and emit the faint smell of lavender countertop spray, and whose eggshell-colored couch is clearly extracted from a West Elm catalog. I wish this was our home, I say to my analyst, and my analyst says, I know. I can picture myself sitting on the couch, drinking coffee and writing, the snow falling outside, my melancholy absorbing the light, a cat curled up beside me. In my phantasy, you are also here, practicing Zen meditation—she points to the opposite side of the open concept living room, where an embroidered patchwork cushion rests on the floor—and at night, we drink wine and workshop our novels, brush our teeth, go to sleep early, wake up, and repeat.

There are no actual cats in our sublet, although in real life, both my analyst and I have Siamese cats we dearly love, living creatures who feel our feelings as deeply as we do. Conversely, in the center of our open concept living room is a dead sheepskin rug with which we both take political offense. Animal rights are a feminist issue, my analyst says. If a person disregards nonhuman animal life, how can he ever respect human life? We are in absolute agreement about the fact that animal rights are entangled with intersectional oppressions, and we assert our mutual position as we drink pink wine and cook tofu pups in a cast iron grill pan. As they heat, the tofu pups form small bubbles and become imbued with grill marks. I can't wait to cover my pup in ketchup, my analyst says. Of course, I feel the same. I am from Pittsburgh, birthplace of the world's most famous ketchup.

My analyst has never been to Pittsburgh, but she wants to go. When she tells me this, I say: We'll plan a trip. My father would love to meet you! There is a new Ace Hotel in the neighborhood where I grew up. The neighborhood has changed a lot. Last year, I watched a video of a bulldozer demolishing a high-rise building in the neighborhood's center. When I was younger, my mother—the waterfowl collector— and I—her ugly ghost—would go shopping in a strip mall across from what is now the bulldozed building. We adopted our first cat in that strip mall. I named her Tess; her coat was black and white. Days after her adoption, I became convinced she was mentally ill, but at that point it was too late to take her back to the shelter. Besides, I could never abandon her: True love is the act of never letting go. Anyway, I take issue with the hyper-gentrification of my old neighborhood, and with the fact that a behemoth tech corporation has colonized my hometown. It's gotten so bad that another tech corporation is currently bidding on the city to host its second headquarters. I would never move back to Pittsburgh, and I have not visited in years, but because you want to go, I'll go. It will be interesting to show you the street on which I grew up. Will it be how you imagine? My father still lives in my childhood home. Across the street from it is a playground. Perhaps we can carve a novel into one of its trees. From the top of one of the playground's turrets, you can see the tallest building in the city. One thing to know about this playground is that it is attached to the Western Pennsylvania School for Blind Children, so you may notice braille on the playground equipment, and occasionally you will see people who cannot see you, or who can only partially see you. Have you read "Blindness" by Jorge Luis Borges? I've always wanted to teach an interdisciplinary disability studies creative writing course called *Writing Without Looking,* but I haven't gotten around to it yet.

In our Hamptons sublet, my analyst and I are disappointed that the ketchup left in our refrigerator by the sublet's previous tenants is not the type of ketchup Ronald Reagan considered a vegetable. Rather, our sublet's ketchup is actually a vegetable, insofar as organic ketchup exists at the bottom of the food pyramid. We reluctantly make this admission to one another: That we both desire to ingest a type of ketchup infused with GMOs and high-fructose corn syrup, and that we—critical thinkers who care deeply about the environment and food politics—feel disappointed in ourselves for desiring that type of ketchup in this way. Upon admitting our shame, we begin laughing. Sometimes, I feel orthorexic, I say. I had a painful relationship to food as a teenager. When my mother and I went out to dinner, I would never remember who I was.

What do you remember?

I remember sitting across from my mother in a vinyl booth at a restaurant whose mascot was a smiley face. She is pushing a plate of chicken toward me. I look at the chicken; it looks at me. Hovering in attention, the chicken becomes part of my body. I imagine its flesh affixed to my right oblique, fattening my stomach, then picture it trapped inside my small intestine, refusing to come out. Next, I am standing outside of myself, holding a plate covered in cubed ham, hard-boiled eggs, and shredded cheese. The restaurant's fluorescent lights flicker and cut to the trunk of a car, where I am naked and being beaten by an older man who—I burst into tears—is now a preacher.

I feel your memory, which is not only a keen recollection, but also a mirror, my analyst says. You articulate the world in a precise synthesis of image and affect, yielding a lyricism so deeply articulated that I cannot help but remember your past as if I exist inside it. The chicken, the cubed ham, the older man—these things happened to me too. They happened to me too.

To accompany our tofu pups, my analyst and I bake tater spuds, a fanciful kind of tater tot sold in the freezer aisle at the Park Slope Food Coop. It's simple, our shared meal, but time gets lost while we eat it, accompanied as we are by a bottle of pink wine, which we imbibe until we lose our senses. In the cups, my analyst tells me about the time she first dropped acid as a freshman at Bennington College. I was seventeen, she says. My birthday fell at the cusp of my elementary school's registration deadline, so I began college earlier than the rest of my peers.

My birthday is September 12th, I say. I was also the youngest in my class.

Carl Jung believed synchronous events are related by meaning, versus causality, my analyst says. Since we first met, I have experienced our connection as paranormal, and the images and events that bind us as uncanny. Our mutual synchronicities disturb the boundaries between the living and the dead, and therefore touch the heart. Per Zen Buddhism, our simultaneity—our shared spiritual insight—awakens us toward truth. In contrast, my first experience on acid was unenlightening. I remember sitting on the green late one Friday night with a group of people with whom I imagined I would be forever friends, but with whom I immediately lost touch upon declaring my major in English. A floppy-haired boy in a Joy Division shirt—at this point in the story, she laughs and says: Joy Division, what symbolism!—lifted a small paper to the end of my tongue. I let it dissolve. As I did, I thought about my parents, who disapprove of recreational drugs but who occasionally reminisce about doing drugs themselves. To my chagrin, I remember my father once recounting how he dropped acid and drove his Volkswagen Bug around a suburban cul-de-sac. He told me every sign on the road seemed to say WRONG WAY—you're going the wrong way—when in fact they said DEAD END.

My trip felt less doomed. It began with what I believe was an homage to *Pinocchio*: I pictured a wooden marionette—genderless and lithe, neither artificial nor real—with no clothes on, into whose torso the following phrases were carved: *LOVEBOT, WORK HARD, HELP*. I approached the marionette, greeted it, and ran my palm over its text before finding myself in a consulting room, which was not unlike the consulting room where we meet. The couch in the consulting room was red, and next to it stood a second marionette, identical to the first. Initially, it stood still, but eventually it began to sway back and forth, as if it were Audrey Horne dancing to her own theme song. Unaccompanied by music, it began moving slowly. By the end of the scene, it appeared to be having a seizure.

For over twenty years, I have been thinking about what the marionette represents. This is a question I can only answer with another question. Because everything I write transforms into reality—it is never the other way around—I have always wondered if the twin marionettes were objects I might encounter in the future, and if the phrases carved into their torsos were letters to myself. For example, *LOVEBOT* seems to suggest I approach attachment as a program. I input linguistic variables into other people to make them attach themselves to me. I input "I love you" into another person, and if the "I love you" program runs successfully, the other person says "I love you too." We should all fall in love less, I think. What we call love is frequently a delusion. And if we were less delusional, we could *WORK HARD*-er, finish our novels, feel more successful than we are. But we never ask for *HELP* when we need it. Maybe if we carved reminders into our flesh, and looked at these reminders every day, and approached their messages with seriousness, and acted in light of their commands, thereby executing our bodies' programs, we would be better teachers, writers, friends. We would be better humans.

You're already a good human, I say. You're a deity.

If I were better, you would be too.

What do you mean?

Sometimes, I think I'm your mirror.

Like the Velvet Underground song?

I love that song, my analyst says, pouring another glass of wine. It's been a long time since I've heard it.

Lou Reed wrote it for Nico, I say. Nico told Lou she would be his mirror, and he wrote "I'll Be Your Mirror" for her to sing.

I'll be your mirror, my analyst sings. Reflect what you are—

—in case you don't know, I sing along.

I'll be the wind, she sings.

The rain and the sunset, we sing. The light on your door—

—to show that you're home, she sings.

When you think the night has seen your mind, we sing.

That inside you're twisted and unkind, we sing.

Let me stand to show that you are blind, we sing.

Please put down your hands, we sing.

…'cause I see you. My analyst points at me and laughs.

I'll be your mirror too, I say. In case you don't know.

My analyst laughs and takes a long, slow sip of wine. As she drinks, the open concept living room's soft light is reflected in the wine's legs, its tears.

Throughout our vacation in the Hamptons, my analyst and I do very little, though part of our doing very little involves meta self-reflexively basking in a hybrid register of guilt and gratitude sparked by our seemingly endless amount of leisure. It's like we're in *Bonjour Tristesse*, my analyst says, referring to the 1954 French novel by Françoise Sagan whose title translates to *Hello Sadness*, which was adapted to film by Otto Preminger in 1958. Like *The Wizard of Oz*, the film adaptation of *Bonjour Tristesse* contains both color and black-and-white sequences. In the film adaptation of the novel, my analyst is most certainly Jean Seberg's character Cécile, a decadent seventeen-year-old trying to break up her father's relationship with Anne, his mistress. And I am one of the extras in the conga line— unremarkable, plain, but having a good time, such a good time. Our minimalist Hamptons sublet—with its open concept living room, organic ketchup, and cast-iron grill pan—is the villa where the film's main characters arrive for a visit.

I can't believe Françoise Sagan wrote *Bonjour Tristesse* when she was only nineteen, my analyst says. Will I ever finish *Kind Mirrors, Ugly Ghosts*?

I have a premonition you will, I say, and when you do, it will be a howling success.

In 2005, a critical theorist named Sianne Ngai wrote a book called *Ugly Feelings*—have you read it? It's an exploration of negative emotions such as envy, anxiety, irritation, paranoia, and disgust. The book's jacket copy describes these feelings as non-cathartic and politically ambiguous, in contrast to a feeling like anger.

My feelings are both angry and ugly—and ambient, related to their surroundings.

Sometimes my feelings become diffuse; sometimes, I think it would be nice if a diffuser existed for feelings: I would put drops of feeling into it like essential oil, and they would spread into thin air.

I read somewhere that when an analysand feels hopeful feelings about her analyst, these hopeful feelings are displaced feelings about herself, so maybe my hopeful feelings about *Kind Mirrors, Ugly Ghosts* are actually feelings I can't have about myself.

I read on Wikipedia that a critic once referred to *Bonjour Tristesse* as "a nice piece of precocity."

That's condescending, I say. No one takes young writers seriously.

I can't bring myself to open my laptop today, my analyst says. I feel sick.

I feel a lack.

Lacan says the lack always relates to desire.

One lack takes up another lack—the real, earlier lack—and the two lacks become desire.

I am thinking now of how to articulate emotion as it occurs in the transference.

Sometimes I think of the word *ambivalence*, but I keep returning to *love*.

Is it possible we free ourselves from one another?

Or that, as one, we become free?

Wikipedia says Deleuze and Guattari say that desire does not arise from lack, but is instead a productive force.

I don't know if I agree, but I appreciate the prosody of Deleuze and Guattari's combined names.

Moi aussi, my analyst says.

Do you want a cup of tea?

I want tea.

It is early Saturday morning. My analyst and I are drinking tea at a Formica kitchen table in the center of a beach, adjacent to white orchids in a terra cotta pot that lean in to say hello. I bought these flowers after one of our sessions, I say. The plants at the Union Square Greenmarket are always the most affordable. This is important, as I am currently practicing a particular form of asceticism. Because I am an adjunct, I must live as austerely as I can. Of course, I broke my ascetic streak last night when I took a private car to my friend's apartment to lay on his bed and watch a British documentary series about the ocean. My friend and I have been watching this documentary series for months. We are obsessed with underwater sex. This is evidenced by the fact that, every time we watch the series, we replay a scene featuring two cuttlefish humping. One cuttlefish attracts the other by camouflaging itself as the other cuttlefish's gender. As my friend and I watch this, we laugh, and our bodies move closer together. But our friendship is not sexual; in fact, my friend is gay. Our closeness defies the chasm created by sex, which doesn't mean we are not each other's person. Indeed, like people who are each other's people, we spend our time eating popcorn and performing domestic tasks: grocery shopping, cooking dinner, doing dishes. Often, we walk to a laundromat, where I watch him run his hands over his wet clothes. Goddamn these fucking machines, he says, referring to the fact that the laundromat's washers do not wring water out of fabric.

The tea my analyst and I drink is made from flowers—chamomile and lavender—and dried peppermint. To prepare this blend, I travelled to the food coop alone and selected the ingredients by myself, individually doled out as they were in small plastic bags to which my analyst and I take offense. If only plastic ceased to exist, we say to each other at the same time. Then the ocean would not be in jeopardy, and the cuttlefish could hump in ecstasy until the end of time—which, like sexuality, is a social construct. Take the ontology of the zebra mantis shrimp, for example. Throughout its life, the male zebra mantis shrimp assumes the role of performing the heteronormative task wherein he provides for the female zebra mantis shrimp who stays at home tending to her eggs, who cannot provide for herself. These shrimp live in deep water, feigning monogamy. The male shrimp stays with the female shrimp for up to twenty years, until he leaves her for another female shrimp.

At which point, the abandoned female shrimp is left to scream in despair until another shrimp comes.

A STORY ABOUT A NAKED GIRL IN A SNOW GLOBE ON THE SHELF OF AN AMERICAN MULTINATIONAL RETAIL CORPORATION

A girl is sitting in a snow globe on the shelf of an American multinational retail corporation. She is naked, and a man restocking the shelf with various other snow globes of divergent shapes, colors, sizes, and styles is studying her body with his penis in lieu of completing his work. He is inspecting the girl to see how naked she is, and to discern whether or not she is naked enough to hold in his mind when she doesn't exist in plain sight. For this man does not possess the ability to engage in object permanence with the women who inhabit his life: his mother, his daughter, his wife. It always seems as if they're there when they're there, and that, when they're gone, he's completely alone: at peace, at long last—and empty, sans women whose needs and desires only serve as distractions.

The girl in the snow globe is also alone, and also empty, and also pornography—she is naked, after all, and was rendered by a fifty-eight-year-old factory worker who compulsively masturbated as he hand-painted her breasts—but because she is enclosed in water in a transparent sphere punctuated by white particles that fall through the water when the globe is shaken, her aloneness induces within her the sorts of existential quandaries typically reserved for a first-year undergraduate composition course. For example, *Recount a time when you faced a challenge, setback, or failure. How did it affect you, and what did you learn from the experience?* Or, *Describe a topic, idea, or concept you find so engaging it makes you lose all track of time. Why does it captivate you? What or who do you turn to when you want to learn more?*

One can see through glass but not water, nor can one not see through water. The snow globe's water doesn't have a color, so something about it feels transparent, or the fluorescent lights of the American multinational retail corporation make it such that when the man who is studying the girl's body with his penis restocks the shelf while looking at the girl, she can't discern whether or not he's a ghost. He may be a pervert, but she may also be in love with him because he is the only man in the store who continuously returns to the snow globe aisle, and it would be fatal to fall in love with anyone who merely browses the snow globes, for those visitors to the aisle rarely return. Take, for instance, the man dressed in a camouflage vest who fingered her snow globe's glass on Christmas Day (the American multinational retail corporation is open on Christmas Day; everything without a heart is). When this man arrived, she became enamored with the whorls and lines of his fingers, which stained the glass within which she resides, and in her enamored state, she thought about entwining her small fingers with his big ones, and experienced this scale of size as erotic, and experienced too a fantasy of breaking through her snow globe's glass to find a ring for his finger in the American multinational retail corporation's jewelry department, but in this fantasy she had no idea how to 1) scale the ring counter to view the ring collection; 2) extract the ring from its case; 3) carry the ring to a secure location containing the man whose name she does not know; and 4) speak, and therefore propose. But the girl in the snow globe is empty and therefore does not experience true desire, and by the time this fantasy had crystallized in her mind, the man was gone. She missed him—or at least imagined she did—but she could not cry in the snow globe because a girl in a snow globe is already contained by water, and tears are also water, thus there is no differentiating them from the snow globe's interior. Nor can one distinguish it from the ocean, where the girl is glued to the floor and can't move her arms or legs, her hands or feet.

IF ANYBODY COULD HAVE SAVED ME IT WOULD HAVE BEEN YOU

She is sitting on the beach eating a chocolate chip cookie housed in a metal canister per the sort of metal canisters she imagines midcentury soldiers' wives packed for their husbands to take to war. The day is hot, and the sun melts not only her and her fellow beachgoers' skin, but also the chocolate chip cookie housed within the metal canister whose history she can only imagine. She touches the melting chocolate chip cookie with her finger, then touches her cell phone's liquid crystal display screen, which therein contains a facsimile of Virginia Woolf's suicide letter written in 1941, just after World War II began.

Dearest, the letter begins. *I feel certain that I am going mad again. I feel we can't go through another of those terrible times. And I shan't recover this time. I begin to hear voices, and I can't concentrate. So I am doing what seems the best thing to do.*

Virginia Woolf did not do the best thing to do in the ocean. Rather, she did it in the River Ouse in Lewes, East Sussex, England. Three miles away, in the nearby village of Rodmell, she and her husband Leonard—to whom her suicide note was addressed—owned a weatherboarded cottage. There, she wrote *Orlando*, *To the Lighthouse*, *The Waves*, *The Years*, *Mrs. Dalloway*. In 1910, thirty-one years before her river death, Virginia Woolf—then Adeline Virginia Stephen—had been institutionalized after attempting suicide twice, once by trying to jump out of a window, and once again by overdosing on veronal. Woolf may have had bipolar disorder, sources purport, but words make things name themselves (a poet once said), and she distrusts that one can precisely language anything one's mind does, seeing as no mind is the same, despite the ways our minds all spin out from time to time.

The waves are now lapping against the shore, and the girl on the beach is re-reading Virginia Woolf's suicide letter with her finger. As was aforementioned, this letter was written to Leonard—her husband, Leonard Woolf, not Cohen nor Bernstein. *If anybody could have saved me it would have been you*, she wrote, reaffirming the myth that anybody can rescue anybody. But maybe love can save—meaning to keep safe, to avoid the need to use, to preserve the soul from damnation—a person, or maybe another person's attention can save another person, or maybe if adults failed to tell us *good job* and *I love you* when we were small, nothing could save us but ourselves.

After reading Virginia Woolf's suicide letter on the beach, whose sand is hot and therefore makes her skin stick to her body, she walks back to the train past the bar where an elderly man is drinking. *Hello sweetheart,* he says, and she winks at him, but he cannot see her eye because it is covered by plastic meant to protect her irises from the sun, and she cannot see what he is drinking because her vision is tinted. On the train, she misses the elderly man, not because he is memorable but because there is no one else to call to mind.

A lie?

A lie.

First, she thinks of her former beloved, and then she thinks of the elderly man. He was sitting at a bar without sitting at the bar, for in fact, he was sitting outside of the bar where he was drinking. Scanning the train with her tinted vision, the girl considers the straight line of energy required for the train's bars to extend from the train's ceiling to its floor, much like the elm tree behind the weatherboarded cottage in a village where she has not yet moved, and which she cannot call to mind because she will not move into the weatherboarded cottage for several months and thus has not yet made its acquaintance. But we know things before we know things, she intuits, and so somewhere within her consciousness she lets herself visualize it and subsequently feels quiet and adrift from her present reality, though she does not let herself know what she knows despite the fact she knows it.

In the past, when she was eating a homemade chocolate chip cookie housed in a metal canister per the sort of metal canisters she imagines midcentury soldiers' wives packed for their husbands to take to war, she did not feel adrift in quite this exact way, nor did she feel out of tune with her consciousness' registers of knowledge. In other words, she did not feel the detachment of her mind from her body, nor did she fear the repercussions of exiting the beach to re-enter the world. Nor did she imagine herself to be anywhere but on the beach, albeit now, writing this, she feels an ocean in her torso, and this ocean provokes her to once again return to the actual ocean, into which she might step without clinging to reality; into which she might wade with the insistence of one who has also made peace with her grief. In this wading, she will let the water carry her away until I, too, am asleep near the bottom of it.

A STORY ABOUT A TURTLE WHO RETREATS INTO HER SHELL AND BECOMES A REAL GIRL

DIEGO ZAYAS

There is a consulting room contained inside the turtle's shell, and the turtle who retreats into it—who becomes a girl inside of it—is neither a psychoanalyst nor a patient. Rather, she is the ghost of shame, beholding herself as one might behold an amethyst. The girl is not drunk, for the consulting room does not hold a liquor license. Rather, it contains a jute rug, an antique lamp, a copy of Serge Leclaire's *Psychoanalyzing: On the Order of the Unconscious and the Practice of the Letter*, a poster of Harmony Korine's 1997 film *Gummo,* and a couch the color of milk.

If you want, the girl says, you can meet me here in person. You can knock on my shell so as to wake me, and whisper *hello*, and attempt to crack a joke, and comment on my nice hand, and join me on the couch for a glass of wine. The previous sentence about the liquor license was not a lie; I snuck this bottle in myself. It made my tote bag heavy. But the wine is light and lovely, and imported from the Loire Valley. If you don't want to drink it, I can brew coffee or make tea instead. It is important for me to let you know that you are safe in my company, and that your boundaries are respected.

As I tell you this, you say, Things will be okay. But I don't know what those things are.

I understand if you need to turtle for a time. Sometimes I turtle too. It's this thing I do when I feel empty.

What does that mean?

I can't tell.

Say it in my ear.

Both the turtle and the girl are unprocessed, but I am enrolled in psychoanalysis, and therefore know myself. I know I desire to exist in listlessness until the end of time. I know I seek boredom forever. I know the turtle may live to be one hundred seventy, whereas the girl may die in fifty years. I know I shall live to be thirty-six. When you think about it, the three of us—the turtle, the girl, and me—are neither old nor young. Rather, we comprise a triptych: three separately framed artworks hanging on a wall, confounding museumgoers.

Love, a wall text says, is always a red herring.

And that much may be true: the word *love* is frequently misused.

People invoke it when they really mean novelty, or beauty, or sex; or even worse, novel sex: scenes in books featuring characters who grope one another. Authors use this word—*love*—because they lack instruction in logical fallacies, wherein *love* is framed as an argument when it is always an epiphany. And I am sick of feeling attached to the wall.

It is morally wrong to cheat on your spouse; why on earth would you do that?
    But what is morality, exactly?
    It's a code of conduct shared by cultures.
    But who writes this code?

Now I will share a brief anecdote. As I compose it, I shall resist employing the conjunction "but":

> Several years ago, I traveled to the zoo with a friend. We were both animal people—activists, though we did not explicitly refer to ourselves as such. On that day, our shared interest was in observing creatures trapped behind glass. We had both recently read Dale Jamieson's "Against Zoos," and had seen him speak at a hybrid science-philosophy conference. *Do fish feel pain* was a question we regularly asked. Confronted with this inquiry, we looked into each other's eyes and laughed. We each possessed two eyes an observer might describe as *intensely curious*.
>
> Approximately an hour or so into our zoo journey, my friend and I found ourselves gazing into a glass enclosure containing one turtle. This turtle was oversized, its shell resembled painted glass, and its head was smooth and wrinkled, invoking a penis. As we considered the turtle's point of view—was it aware of its lifespan?, we wondered aloud; was

it aware of its containment behind glass?—my friend uttered the word *abject*.

Abject!

I felt in love.

Indeed, I felt my friend. I felt a feeling creeping up on him. And I felt this feeling too. Days later, lying facedown on the floor while stretching my right leg, I was revisited by the feeling, to which I may refer in retrospect as an epiphany. I thought: My friend has a back, and that back has a spine, and if he was assuming my shape on the floor at this moment in time, I would run my hand across it—*it*, the pronoun referring to his spine, smooth while simultaneously containing notches. Then, I fantasized, I would cook him soup, gift him a plant clipping from my plant clipping collection, and take off his shell. Which may not be love—for love is, in fact, the clarifying and sometimes violent process of gazing into strangers' eyes and discerning whose grief feels like one of your fingers.

Will you touch my hand?

Which one.

I speculate that the above explanation does no justice to my exploration of love as a contemporary fallacy, or to my excavation of how the misuse of this word causes me to retreat into the turtle, whose consulting room is an extraordinary space, a room with no view where a girl feels wholly contained. Look at her lying on the couch: she is copulating with the ceiling! Notice as she drifts in and out of her body like the ghost I am, and observe her observing me observing myself observing her detached reality from an aerial perspective. Her stomach rises and falls with the fluctuation of her breath. It makes my hair curl.

Eventually, the real girl will see herself in paper. This material is not reflective, but it is a mirror, for anything you write on it looks you in the face. Because the turtle and I see ourselves in one another, we must be paper too. In this sentence, we are writing one another by addressing you. See how easily we redefine ourselves? Now it's your turn.

CAPTIVE FATHER

I am going to write you a Captive Father. He is two-dimensional, so you can draw clothing for him. You can hold him up to the window—hold paper up to his flat body—hold a marker up to his penis—and trace his waist and legs and draw him jeans. These jeans are black, Captive Father's favorite color.

Captive Father loves to sing along with The Smiths. As you both listen to "Stretch Out and Wait," he tells you about his first sexual encounter. He describes it as the saddest night on Earth. I was young, he says. I didn't know better. And although you feel uncomfortable, you laugh together. And so it comes to pass that when you trace Captive Father's arms and chest—when you draw two sleeves and a crewneck—you are, in fact, preparing to draw Captive Father a shirt emblazoned *Hatful of Hollow*, an adjective denoting an empty space inside, a pregnant void, a lack.

When I write Captive Father, you will always have enough! Because he is a doll, you can keep him in your nightstand. You can design a little room for him there, replete with a cardboard bed padded with cotton balls for extra comfort, a good night's rest. You can cut out miniature CDs from a Columbia House advertisement in a vintage *Rolling Stone* so Captive Father will always have The Smiths. And I will gift you a miniature Bible and a miniature dictionary, so Captive Father will always have a pair of books to read. Subsequently, you will cut images out of fashion magazines and affix them to the walls: Coco Chanel, Alexander McQueen, Oscar de la Renta.

In Captive Father's nightstand, you will find a set of miniature condoms for him to wear while he is having sex. And he is always having sex, Captive Father. He is having it with boys, his way, as boys tend to like it. And now you may be wondering: What color is the carpet? The carpet, I posit, is the color of reneging on the world, and of obfuscation, and workaholism, and secrets. The truth is, everyone has something to hide, wherein *hide* denotes the skin of an animal. The condoms may be crafted from sheep, or lamb, or latex. They may be pink, or red, or green, or any color of the rainbow. The floors in Captive Father's room may be hardwood or carpet. Which texture do you prefer? I want Captive Father's dresser drawer room to feel like a home, like the home you never had. While you are at work, I want you to be able to picture Captive Father comfortably sprawled out across his cotton ball bed, reading his miniature dictionary, utterly at peace. I want you to know Captive Father will be there when you get back. All you have to do is close the drawer. From inside, he cannot open it. While you are gone, he will sit in the dark and stare at the glow in the dark stars you have affixed to his walls, and imagine Orion, and pretend each star is a literary work within a constellation clustered around a particular theme—for example, nonhuman utopias, or queer ecologies, or kissing architectures. Computational linguistics, perhaps, or Lacanian psycho-analysis, or the poetics of every affect known to man: rage, love, shame, abandonment, illness, self-harm, estrangement. When you want him to look tough, you can dress Captive Father in a black sweater and boots, and cook him mushrooms to strengthen his immune system from the inside. Be aware, however, that Captive Father is flat. He is made of paper. He has no intestines, so he never has to relieve himself of anything.

MY EX-PARTNER'S DOPPELGÄNGER

Once a month, I take a walk with my ex-partner's doppelgänger, a graphic designer with whom I share a checkout shift at my local food cooperative. At the food cooperative, my ex-partner's doppelgänger and I cooperate with one another. *Can you bring this cart back to its vestibule*, I ask my ex-partner's doppelgänger, who pushes the cart away from the register where I scan and bag strangers' groceries. During lulls in service, my ex-partner's doppelgänger stands next to my register, offering me blueberries. It has become routine, this offering of blueberries. *I was thinking about your blueberries earlier today*, I tell my ex-partner's doppelgänger, and extract a blueberry from its plastic shell. As I place the blueberry in my mouth, I think about microplastics getting caught in fishes' gills and, in my mind, envision a fish—a carp, tilapia, or mackerel; a haddock, cod, or rainbow trout—washed up on a sandy shoreline. Its colorful likeness, encumbered by the micro-plastics, is captured from above, as if by camera drone. Its eyes face skyward. How will it find the ocean? Via this question, a foreboding melancholia plagues me. This feeling feels at odds with the blueberry's bright hue. As I blow the little brain out of my mind's fish, I cannot perceive whether my despair is in response to its dead meat, or in response to my killing it. Nor do I imagine my ex-partner's doppelgänger possesses the sort of interior sensitivity that might attune him to this quandary. For the sensitivity I possess is as rare as hen's teeth: most days, I smell the past or taste the dead and am awash with grief.

On our walks, which span approximately twenty blocks, my ex-partner's doppelgänger tells me about his family. In it, there is one mother, and one father, although these two archetypes are no longer married to one another. One archetype—the mother—is now married to someone else. My ex-partner's doppelgänger does not care for the mother's new partner. Together, we commiserate. What else is there to do but bitch? *I have to go home for Christmas*, my ex-partner's doppelgänger says, and I squeeze his hand with my eyes, because he will not let me touch it. This is because my ex-partner's doppelgänger is devoted to a life partner who makes demands on his attention, and so too demands his sexual exclusivity. And this demand is fine by me. I no longer want to fuck just anybody. That period of my life is complete. I am in a new period, wherein I desire to walk down familiar streets with someone unbeknownst to me, beginning at one point and ending at the next, as if we are attempting to draw a line between the past and a future with our bodies. When I attempt to draw these lines alone, the lines do not exist. Only in the company of my ex-partner's doppelgänger is the passage of time real.

DAVID

I am on a beach in Southern California holding my mother. We are lying on a beach towel; my head rests on her chest. It is sunset. The sky is orange and pink and gold, the color of the rainbow sherbet I ate as a child during our "ice cream walks" to Baskin-Robbins. The sky's pink swirls and drips against our best wishes, in what feels like an unnatural climate doom-induced hue:

Aware that California will be wiped away before I ever have the chance to visit, I say to my mother: "I wish things could last forever."

To which she replies: "They can't."

/

In a dream, I am lying on the floor of a pink-walled room with David, a stranger I met on the Internet. The pink is Baker-Miller, a tone used to calm prisoners in their cells, and the room's lighting is dim. I can see David's face, trapped behind a screen, but I cannot recall what it looks like. Nor do I know why I am lying with him.

I found David on a hook-up website and have not met with him in person. He's said he fantasizes about meeting me at a hotel and once asked me to a drink, both of which I've refused. Instead, he sends me photographs of himself in loungewear and athletic hooded sweatshirts, and I send him photographs of my breasts. This is my preferred method of sexual intercourse.

David makes me nervous, so he makes me feel secure—or, if nothing else, David feels familiar. Like me, he is self-protective, skittish, unpredictable. He says what he wants with an authoritative tone that reminds me of a Catholic school principal. *Send me a photograph of your breasts*, he commands, and I do. He says my eyes in the photograph appear troubled and in heat, a description that turns me on. Yet what turns me on the most about David is that when I move toward him, he backs away, retreating as one does into the waters of digital technology. Love is a game of hide and seek, after all—so says D.W. Winnicott, a dead pediatrician and psychoanalyst. And here on the floor of my unconscious, we swim toward one another—David and I—trapped as we are between death and waking life, three-dimensional reality and the flat waters of our screens.

I'm addicted to renting pornographic tapes at the adult video store by my apartment, David texts.

To which I respond: *Adult video stores still exist?*

To care is inherently anxious. One applies care only after one has been forced to learn carefulness. *Carefully* is an adverb one balances on a spoon while walking. *Careful* is an adjective one assumes in relation to another person's unpredictable patterns of behavior. *Caring* is a verb that wears a guise of benign temperament to conceal its cracked interior. When a person finds herself in a situation where caring for someone else might jeopardize her heart, she retreats into her shell, and forms a protective field around her body, an invisible barbed wire razor ribbon fence no one can touch without getting cut.

As a barbed wire razor ribbon fence-clad turtle in water, I swim toward David, ready to slice off his face.

On the seventh day of my companionship with David, I learn to clip Woebegone's nails. Woebegone is my new tortoiseshell cat, so she is also a turtle. Her coat is peanut butter and black, with small patches of white scattered throughout. One common misconception about Woebegone is that I named her after a lake. This is false. I named her after sadness.

By now, I am calling Woebegone a nickname—Woebe—as well as several pet names: Woebegoon; Woebegeezer; warm buddy; fuzzy friend; little mama; petite maman; and baby Woe. At night, Woebe sleeps on a silk pillowcase, curled up against my skull, occasionally twitching and biting my nose. After several hours, she burrows into the comforter and rests her head on my chest, as if she were a child sleeping with her mother. When she gnaws my fingers, does she also think my fingers are her mother's nipples? And if David were to gnaw my breasts, would he think the same?

In my dream journal, I write: *I keep having dreams wherein everyone I've ever loved is my mother. In these dreams, there is no father. Always we are lying in bed, clutching each other's hair.*

In a photograph he sends me, David is looking at his wristwatch with a surprised expression on his face. In this JPEG, he looks like a comic book character, with two actual eyes, big glasses, and layer upon layer of clothing, including his black athletic sweatshirt, tucked under a jacket over which his hood protrudes. He is wearing a name tag on his lapel that says *David* (Why is David wearing a name tag in his workout clothes? Does he work at a gym?). There is a mirror in the background, reflecting an electronic keyboard, a rack of weights, and David.

David used to be thin; now, like a horse, he is muscular, athletic.

If he were a letter of the alphabet, he says, he would be the letter H: a ladder with only one rung, or two first-person pronouns connected by a dash—David and *David*. This is why David does not need me: he is already two. But who, in three-dimensional reality, is David?

The mirror does not answer.

David does not play piano; he does not make art; he does not go to the movies, or museums, or the grocery store. He does not drink; he does not eat meat; he does not work; he does not write books. Instead, he sits in his apartment, "in-between jobs" (he says—so why the nametag?) where, all day, he watches pornography. *All I think about is fantasy and sex*, David says when I accidentally seek emotional support from him on the seventh day of our companionship— although *companionship* is an inappropriate noun to apply to our duet. A cat named Woebegone gives me companionship, warmth, unconditional love, and care. In the seven days we have known one another, David has given me scraps.

Not only is love a game of hide and seek; it is a compost heap. Strangers arrive and toss their shit into your pile, and you hope something blooms: a sunflower, a tomato stalk, a melon. *I have no idea how to respond to that*, David says to me when I tell him what I am eating for dinner: gluten-free macaroni and cheese, as prepared from a box. *You don't have to say anything*, I say to David. *I'm sending you a postcard from my life*. To which David responds: *I had a stalker; I went to therapy to deal with her violation of my boundaries. Most likely, I have PTSD. You're making me anxious.*

David's invocation of PTSD makes me pity him, which makes me love him, for I identify with pitiable creatures: convicts, orphans, lice. *You're making me anxious:* I press my finger down upon and heart this message. Then I put my phone on airplane mode and into a drawer and imagine David alone in the two-dimensional battle-field of his screen. In my imagination, which functions akin to his pornographic video tapes, I picture David receiving text message after text message from his stalker, a stranger who did not relate to his avoidance the way I do. After all, I have seen *Wings of Desire*. I understand David is protecting himself in a black-and-white universe that will, with enough effort on my behalf, turn into color. Not that I plan to exert effort. But if I did, all I would need to do to impress David would be to demonstrate my trapeze artistry. I would also need to speak fluent French and become flexible and thin. I would need to study musician Nick Cave's covertly Christian oeuvre, temporarily take up residence in a trailer, flirt with men around a bonfire, and begin drinking again. These days, however, I am focused only on myself and Woebe.

One year ago, I put down an elderly cat named Brix, who was gray and skeletal and had green-globe eyes and long fur I liked to vacuum. She lived to be eighteen, and mirrored my coming-of-age. So when Brix died, so did my coming-of-age.

Deciding to adopt a new cat was not an easy process. I looked at a lot of them on a website that felt akin to the hook-up website via which I first sent David my breasts. There are so many orphan kitties in this world, and not enough resources for them to get spayed or neutered. This results in a serious cat overpopulation issue not unlike that of human beings. As someone who has never felt inclined to bear children, I am happy I can raise a cat, which cannot be compared to a human baby. They are completely different. Though I still call Woebe *Woebaby* and *Baby Woe*.

Woebe's initial presence in my apartment was destabilizing and conjured Brix's ghost. I cried for three days—intensely and relentlessly, and without peace—and even considered bringing her back to the website where I hooked up with her. After I sang Woebe a welcome song through tears on her first evening in my apartment, she began exploring—first sniffing the bathroom walls, then the pink and orange chairs in my living room, followed by the wooden coffee table and the pale blue couch. As Woebe sniffed my apartment like a task, I sat on the floor and continued to weep, wishing she would die.

In the weeks following her adoption, Woebe and I established a routine. Our shared rituals meant I no longer desired for her to disappear. Rather, I began to adore her. In the morning and at night, I fed her a quarter cup of dry food (organic deboned chicken and turkey meal) in a small white bowl featuring a cartoon illustration of a cat. Throughout the day, I also paid attention to ensure her mint green water bowl—handmade in Japan and emblazoned with navy blue flowers—was always clean and full. During our shared free time, I exercised her using a catnip mouse dangling from a metal thread attached to a glitter rod. She leapt into the air like a volleyball player or Olympic gymnast and never seemed to lose energy. When I tired of these combined activities, I plugged photographs of Woebe into an online JPEG-to-ASCII art generator:

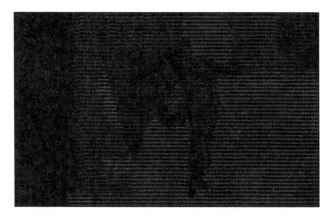

I saved the generator's output to my desktop, and at least thrice daily admired the careful punctuation of my cat.

Woebe and I also appreciate watching reality television programs together. In particular, we love a haunting episode of *Celebrity Wife Swap* starring late actor Verne Troyer, his girlfriend Brittney, and his girlfriend's son, Tyson, who recently passed away. In the episode, Brittney moves into former professional football player Hines Ward's mansion, and Ward's wife moves into Troyer's modest home. Due to conflicting socioeconomic statuses, the wife swap does not go well, and the episode concludes in a disconcerting moral confrontation about affluence and negligent parenting. For weeks, I obsessively rewatched the episode with Woebe by my side, and imagined how its protagonists—Verne Troyer and Brittney, specifically—felt about their failed swap. Did they see their appearance on the show as a form of public humiliation? To help myself better answer this question, I also watched a pornographic video wherein Troyer rides a naked woman (not Brittney) while elevator music plays. A cursory Google search reveals that this tape was originally circulated through adult video stores. In the video's foreground, a candle burns. At one point, Troyer places his head between the naked woman's breasts and lets out a small moan. It is unclear whether his moan is one linked to coming or crying. *Are you okay,* the woman asks. She looks at the camera. Then Troyer kisses her vagina, but not for too long.

Woebegone identifies as a schizoid. She lacks empathy, she says, although she understands the concept in the abstract. She is emotionally aloof and avoids people; she lives alone with me and seldom lets anyone into our apartment. Although I believe her, I know she is not telling the truth. Our relationship is different from Woebe's past ones—of this, I am aware. I bring out Woebe's softer sides, blur her edges until her being dissolves into a boundary-less narrative of faults, a pool of grief at which she finds herself in the center. There, I swim to her, and take her paw, and hold her, and kiss her forehead, and gently scratch her ears, and with this care on my behalf, all manners of Woebe's aloofness fall away, and she begins to purr. *It's okay*, I say, still holding her. *I'm here.* And in this moment, I experience what it feels like to be a mother, though I will never be a mother. I am barren in my solitude, and the world is almost over.

THE RUNAWAY BUNNY

I want to feel close and very far away, my mother says.
Close and far away is what I want too, I say.
Maybe I have intimacy problems, she says.
Maybe I do too.

/

I keep having dreams wherein everyone I've ever loved is my mother. In these dreams, there is no father. Always we are lying in bed, clutching each other's hair.

/

The flying rabbit does not have a mom-tree. He wants to flee, but is flying toward my heart. His fight-or-flight response is a physiological reaction triggered by unconscious memories. This reaction begins in the amygdala, which triggers a neural response in the hypothalamus. Next, the pituitary gland is activated and secretes ACTH, the adrenocorticotropic hormone. Almost simultaneously, the adrenal gland is activated via the sympathetic nervous system, and adrenaline is released into his body. The confluence of these chemical messengers produces cortisol, which increases his blood pressure and weakens his immune system. These reactions are his body's way of trying to boost energy, but instead of feeling energized, he pains and flushes; his heart accelerates; his digestion slows; his pupils dilate; blood vessels constrict; hearing becomes lost; tunnel vision sets in. His spine is disinhibited. I begin shaking.

The Zen monk says when we get curious about our negative emotions—shame, anxiety, jealousy, anger, and so forth—we extend our empathetic capacity, making room for love. And so it is with trepidation that I language my fear, shaking like a leaf. *There's something I haven't said*, I say. *And I don't know how to say it*, I say. *And in my not-saying, I'm finding the words.* All the while, the rabbit flying toward my heart wants to fly away, but instead moves from within—where he was trapped in a box—onto the surface of my flesh.

Now my rabbit is no longer trapped in a box. Instead, he is a bunny with wings, hovering in the air, the element in the center of my name. In lieu of Claire, my mother used to call me *petit lapin rose*—or *little pink rabbit* in French, my dead first language—an image that invokes the eponymous protagonist in Margaret Wise Brown's 1942 children's book *The Runaway Bunny*, he who is pink and white and has two wings via which to fly away from she who finds him every time. *If you become a bird and fly away from me*, she says, *I will be a tree you come home to.* In this conditional sentence, she is both you and I, bunny and bark, bird and house, a warmth that moves up the spine, collaborating with the ribs to form a cage that protects the heart, but does not shield it.

11:11

Having grown up in a Catholic household with a closeted gay parent during the height of the AIDS crisis, I am disgusted with stained glass and ornaments, androgynous angels, three-dollar candles, consecrated water, and the Holy Spirit, the Son, and the Father. When I daydream, I like to imagine I was not three years old in 1989—the year ACT UP protested John Cardinal O'Connor's stance on AIDS—but rather twenty-six or twenty-eight or thirty, or any age that would have allowed me to stand on a wooden pew and shout "SILENCE EQUALS DEATH" into St. Patrick's Cathedral's Gothic revival architecture. I imagine myself lying face down in the center of the church with my fellow protestors, and am subsequently carried out on a stretcher because I refuse to stand. "112 Held in St. Patrick's AIDS Protest," *The New York Times*' headline reads, wherein the headline's original number—111—is increased by one—111 + 1—thereby invoking 11:11, an auspicious number signaling a spirit presence.

COUSINS

A woman and her ex-partner were together for ten years but never married, despite their shared affinity for *The New York Times* Vows column, which appears on Sundays in the newspaper's Style section. Every weekend, they would read Vows aloud to one another—idyllic short stories of couples meeting, falling in love, getting engaged, and marrying, presented sans red flags or conflict. Any real interpersonal turbulence was smoothed over to the pitch of a PG-rated romantic comedy movie. They cut out their favorites and neatly stacked them on a shelf in their shared office, and fantasized that they, too, would one day get married and submit their wedding announcement for consideration as a *New York Times* Vow.

One Sunday evening, after the woman had gone grocery shopping at the food coop, she walked in on her ex-partner taking a shower with a younger woman she had never seen. The younger woman was running one hand through her ex-partner's thick, black, curly hair while simultaneously jerking his penis off with her other hand. Their clothes—a black fabric pile of assorted textures and shapes—were heaped on the bathroom floor like a mass grave. As the woman gazed at her ex-partner's naked body co-mingling with that of the younger woman, a naked sculpture of an otherworldly baby with huge celestine-colored eyes and a massive erection was displayed on a plinth in the living room behind her.

Later, as they were breaking up, the woman's ex-partner would explain that he had met the younger woman, Adrian, on a hook-up website. With an anxious but ultimately sociopathic smile on his face, he explained to the woman that he had lied to Adrian and told her he was in an open marriage.

"But we aren't even married," she said.

"We might as well be. Our partnership feels too close, too much like family. From this point on," he said, "It will be better for us to be friends."

/

A man I met on a hook-up website visited my apartment to eat grouper. He wore a black sweater and black pants and had a head and a face, unlike his profile picture, which only captured his half-naked body from the neck down. He had a crooked smile, a Roman nose, and the phrase *LOVE AFTER PAIN* tattooed on his left hand. His hair was also black, and curly and thick. I wondered if his pubic hair was too, though our intention was to develop an emotional connection before crossing any sexual boundaries. I set this parameter in order to remain in control, but I could not help but fantasize about losing it—a pattern I tend to repeat when I seek out short-term relationships.

As we sat at my kitchen table and ate, the man talked about his outsider art collection, his penchant for sacred harp music, his cottage upstate, and his woodworking practice. How did he have money for a cottage upstate? Although he was not wearing a wedding ring on his left finger, he eventually began to talk about his wife, whom he ecstatically called "my wife." "I'm a very bad husband," he said. "I cheat on my wife all the time." At least he wasn't lying about being in an open marriage!

There was a way the man expressed his self-loathing while cutting the grouper that was unusually beguiling. He sliced the fish as if he were harming it by running his knife through its center—which would be the case if the grouper were still alive, as neurobiologists confirm that fish have nervous systems and respond to pain. Earlier that day, I read about the practice of catch-and-release fishing on PETA's website, wherein a fish is caught by a fisherman before it is let go. So states the website: "Catch-and-release fishing is cruelty disguised as sport." But the National Park Service's website claims otherwise. "In catch and release fishing anglers immediately release native fish—unharmed—back to the water where they are caught," it says. "When done correctly, catch and release methods result in high survival rates."

Upon observing his cutting style, I told the man all of this, then looked down at my own half-eaten dead fish seasoned with lemon, chili pepper, ginger. It was covered in translucent juices and smelled briny and sweet, like the ocean or freshly cut grass.

Before the man, who looked uncomfortable that I had just said a lot about the ethics of killing fish, could respond to my inquisition, I asked: "Does your wife have a name?"

/

My first pet was a betta fish named Rudy. I don't remember where I adopted him. He was the color of menstrual blood, with a spectacular fin display that resembled flower petals. I liked to sit and watch him swim laps across the fish tank, from one glass wall to the next, and then back and forth again, as if he were competing in the 1992 Summer Olympics. I was six years old then, and although Rudy was ageless and couldn't express pain, we became two lonely creatures inhabiting a room devoid of anything but moving images of swimmers competing in their lanes. They aired live on the television next to us.

Today, there exists an activist group who protests the trade and sale of betta fish. I know this because I frequently walk through the Union Square Greenmarket after psychoanalysis. One afternoon, I heard a protest—the sound of voices through bullhorns—emanating from Petco, a store located near the upper northwest region of the Greenmarket. Upon closer inspection, I observed a group of demonstrators holding cardboard signs containing enlarged photographs of betta fish, brightly colored and highly territorial fighting fish who exhibit aggression toward one another if housed in the same tank. In my memory, the text printed on the activists' signs declared something like "STOP PETCO." But words are only rendered animate by the subjects carrying them. When they cease to exist in print and are consequently disposed of (on cardboard posters or 8 ½ by 11-inch sheets; on paper napkins or used receipts), their meanings drift away, and only energetic traces of the alphabet remain. Yet words want to be alive, they crave oxygen, and they possess an uncontrollable desire to feed. Analogously, before he transformed into light, Rudy existed in a tank where, as a form of protest, he consumed all his companion fish. He dominated them, ate them up, then left them to die at the water's surface. What more can be written? He wanted the tank to himself.

/

One week later, I walked three blocks and descended a concrete staircase toward a subway platform where I awaited a train that would take me to see a movie. My phone had recently fallen into the shower and suffered water damage, much to my chagrin. While I awaited the arrival of a replacement phone, I could not readily browse the hook-up website where I had recently met a lovely, married environmental lawyer with thick, black, curly hair. He reminded me of my ex-partner with whom I no longer speak. Even though I had entered into our arrangement with a casual encounter in mind, I always became a spigot of grief following his departures. For days, I would cry and cry and cry, awaiting his return. Now drained from crying and sans the presence of my phone, I possessed electric energy. I was porous, like a human quartz or sponge.

And so it happened, as I descended the concrete staircase and walked toward the subway platform, that I made eye contact with an alien with neon hair the color of a tropical fish whose face was strangely contorted. One side of it did not seem to move, while the other side was animated. His features created a lack of symmetry despite the fact that his eyes, bright blue as celestite, were aligned. His arms were covered in tattoo sleeves, and one of his forearms was concealed in black ink, a redaction or form of self-censorship.

Noticing our eye contact, the alien walked toward me. When we stood face-to-face, he paused.

"Did you ever work at a pet store?" he said.

"No," I said, holding open the book I was reading about Zen Buddhism and the cessation of craving.

"That's funny," he said. "You look like the love interest from *Rocky*."

My heart pounded.

"You're even skittish like her," he said.

I nervously laughed. "I have not seen the movie," I said, and a train passed underground. It was very loud, and I was thankful for its sound, hoping that I would not have to continue talking to this alien.

"You have not seen *Rocky*," the alien repeated back at me. "The character that looks like you is very pretty and takes care of turtles at the pet store."

To which I did not respond.

And then the alien asked me: "Do you like marijuana?"

A second train passed, breathing a sound of relief. I motioned my hand in a gesture meant to communicate the French phrase *comme ci, comme ça*, although it had been some time since I had consumed marijuana, and I did not want to be communicating with this man who had permeated my boundary, which was perhaps not a boundary but an invisible wall between myself and others, destabilizing my sense of self and leaving me receptive to the world and its aliens—which is what this man was: a very high alien. And the fact of this alien's predation was not a fact but a feeling in me. It is not what happens in the mind that counts, but rather how one relates to the happening. And in this happening, I was not relating. I was withdrawing into my shell, O skittish turtle whom I tend at the pet store.

"Give me a second," the alien said, and he subsequently walked to a black trash can and spit in it. As he spit, I turned my head, first to the left, then to the right. There was a boy beside me whom I am calling a boy because he looked younger than I, although this boy was of course a young man. He was wearing a black sweater and black pants and had a head and a face. His hair was also black, and curly and thick, and I wondered if his pubic hair was too.

"Help me," I mouthed.

The young man took out his headphones, was now also porous.

"Can you help me?" I mouthed.

The young man nodded and took my arm. "You're my cousin," he said, and walked me toward the front of the subway platform. The fact that he called me his cousin made me feel a transcendent sense of inner calm and security: cousins protect each other. Nevertheless, the alien was walking behind us, following us toward the front of the train car. As we walked together, my new cousin told me his name, which I cannot recall. Was it Cameron, an anagram for *romance*, or Edward, derived from the Old English meaning *prosperous guardian*?

"Where are you going tonight, Cameron or Edward?" I said.

"I'm going to a concert," he said.

The alien began to yell incoherently, his voice echoing through the subway station.

"I'm taking myself to a movie," I said.

"Oh," he said. "Which movie?"

DONNIE DARKO

On October 31, 2018, I let Frank come into my apartment. Until Frank, my apartment was a shield, a vest no bullet could penetrate, but because he wore all black and deodorant that smelled like a high school locker room; and grinned in a way that calls to mind the verb "to groom"; because he was married but did not wear a ring; because he possessed a seductive, flat affect; because he used wheatpaste to inspire the populace to rise; because he had fine taste in contemporary sculpture; because he purported to be a fiction writer while, in fact, he wrote nothing beyond sexually suggestive emails; and because he attended Zen meditation regularly, asked questions about my emotional landscape, cared for a few houseplants, and did not tell me about his wife until four months into our friendship, I drank two glasses of wine with him in my living room and made small talk, and came to terms with the inevitability of certain events to come.

"Do you like Joy Division," I asked Frank, pointing to an *Unknown Pleasures* poster across the room. The historical reference to concentration camp brothels in juxtaposition with his extramarital encounter was not lost on me. As I sat on the couch with Frank, succumbing to each necessary step leading to sexual intercourse (the red wine, the wide eyes, the pillar candle, etcetera), I thought about how I wished I had married my ex-partner of twelve years when he wanted to marry me, and how, if we had gotten married, I would have worn my *Unknown Pleasures* t-shirt to the tenth floor of City Hall on the day of our elopement. There, one half of a gay couple waiting to exchange their vows would have made an allusion to the first song on *Unknown Pleasures*, "Disorder"—"On the tenth floor, down the back stairs, it's a no man's land," one of the men would have said—and I would have experienced the spirit moving through me, though I would have been unable to metabolize the feeling.

Until Frank entered my life, processing my feelings was impossible. Sometimes, my feelings were ambient, like a record I chose from a shelf and placed on my turntable, to which I would listen while lying in bed with my eyes closed. Other times, they were floating sheets, ghosts of ghosts of ghosts I did not know I knew, and so I could not touch them. Always, they were concentrated, and I would think about how nice it would be if a diffuser existed for them: I would drop them in like essential oils and they would spread into thin air.

Frank, a two-way mirror, introduced me to my rage. Looking into his eyes, I would not see myself, but rather a camera filming me, dutifully projecting my gaze back onto his face's disembodied monitor, so I too appeared inside the monitor, where I would present my palm back to my own gaze, which I pressed to the screen of Frank's face. When my palm touched Frank, time rippled. Then Frank would gaze at me, his teeth situated beneath his ears, and press back. "How can you do that," I asked, to which Frank did not respond.

A website devoted to demystifying everything explains that there are five ways to determine whether a person in front of you is a two-way mirror. First, you must observe whether they are hanging on a wall, or whether they are part of the wall itself. If a person seems to be part of a wall, there is a good chance they are two-way. Second, observe their lighting. Look around and consider whether their light is extraordinarily bright. Next, consider where you are. Note that it is illegal to become a two-way mirror in private spaces; however, in several states, it is legal for dressing rooms to contain surveillance cameras. Finally, do things such as: tap on the surface of the person, place your fingernail against him, or consider the extreme act of punching his face.

As I recall having unprotected sex with Frank—his decision, not my own, although a person generally possesses some agency in the situations into which she gets herself (and I had gotten myself into this, I convinced myself)—I thought of violence, sexual slavery, the replacement of dead women with more soon-to-be-dead women, and Joy Division's song "No Love Lost," which appropriates language from *House of Dolls*, the 1955 novella by Ka-Tsetnik 135633, a prisoner held at Auschwitz:

> *Through the wire screen*
> *The eyes of those standing outside looked in at her*
> *As into the cage of some rare creature in a zoo*
> *In the hand of one of the assistants*
> *She saw the same instrument*
> *Which they had that morning*
> *Inserted deep into her body*
> *She shuddered instinctively*

Daniella—the protagonist in *House of Dolls*—and other women in the Joy Divisions, concentration camp brothels, ultimately have organs removed from their bodies. In the book, these organs are depicted as missing pieces of the women, hearts floating in jars in doctors' offices, "uprooted chunks of life" that will go on living, while the gaps in women's bodies are replaced by artificial parts.

Before my twenty minutes with Frank was up, I too had a heart.

Before we had sex, Frank and I kissed. I used my tongue; I gripped his neck; I became liquid; then I got scared. Frank's eyes were white; his ears were long; his teeth occupied too much space on his face, extending from the uppermost quadrant of his left jaw to the uppermost quadrant of his right. His forehead glistened, covered in veins. Fear, which coursed through my body, caused my heart to sound like a warning bell, but although I heard it, I ignored it, much in the way a person who hears a fire alarm in the background of her life tends to disregard it. What was it—my heart—trying to say? Abruptly, Frank took off my pants, then his, then looked into my face, filming it. *Why are you wearing that stupid rabbit suit*, I thought, and my heart no longer thumped in my breast. Rather, it was now pounding in the narrow bed. "Why are you wearing that stupid woman suit," Frank said. To which I said nothing.

In lieu of further narrating this scene, I will now describe what I should have done instead of what actually happened. Life's central questions are typically ones of fantasy versus trauma, and in this case, I possess enough self-confidence to assert how I should be the one to rewrite my fate. Therefore, it is with a sense of retribution that I state how, after he called me a *stupid woman*, I turned Frank over onto his back, then stood up on the bed, then stood up on him, and crushed his sternum. Indeed, I lifted my left leg onto his body first, followed by my right, and placed all my weight into the moment. When Frank was no longer breathing, I took one of the medical instruments in my house—a scalpel blade—and drew a heart into his chest. Perhaps I should have extracted the organ right then and there, but instead I took a large houseplant potted in terra cotta and cracked it over his skull. Imagine! A man bleeding in bed from a blow to the head via a houseplant. I laugh thinking about the image of Frank's blood intermingling with soil; soil staining my white cotton comforter; the white cotton comforter forgiving itself for being part of the scene. Then I imagine I put on a record—there are always so many to choose from, but I chose *Unknown Pleasures;* I always choose *Unknown Pleasures*—and tied Frank's hands together in front of his navel using kitchen twine.

After the scene, I call my sister and cry. I am alone in the living room, sitting under strings of Christmas lights, unshowered, once again wearing pants. I can feel Frank's ego inside me; I can feel him entering my apartment. I want to rid myself of him but do not know how; I want to dispose of his body but know it is already gone; I want to write down the facts but know there are none. I also desire to make a gynecological appointment and do so using an online scheduling platform, although it is Halloween, and I am supposed to be at a party with my friends, where I will eat a chocolate chip cookie with butter in it, despite being dairy-free and not knowing where the cookie came from. Did Frank's wife send it to me as a form of punishment?

As I cry on the phone, I stare into my laptop, refreshing Frank's social media page, where there exists no trace of his wife—Frank's poor wife—and I think about whether I too will one day be married to a man who moves through the world without a ring. Then I think about whether I will ever have sex again, and in this moment, it does not seem like it, although it crosses my mind that sex is included on Maslow's hierarchy of basic needs. In fact, a friend recently told me, two male twins once had sex with each other because they needed it. So what if I did too? My encounter with Frank felt like consumption, an infectious bacterial disease characterized by the growth of nodules in the lungs that causes approximately three million deaths each year in developing countries. Its spread is combatted by vaccination and the pasteurization of milk, but I am dairy-free: I identify with cows. They roam pastures and are sacred in certain cultures, but are also victims themselves. I know this because I attended high school with boys who drove to barren fields to tip them over.

Sometimes, men try to impress women by saying they're vegan, and by noting they don't drink cow's milk due to rape. *Is Your Food a Product of Rape?* reads the title of a subpage on PETA's website. So states the website's copy: *Cows produce milk for the same reason that humans do: to nourish their young. In order to force them to produce as much milk as possible, farmers typically impregnate cows every year using a device that the industry calls a "rape rack." To impregnate a cow, a person jams his or her arm far into the cow's rectum in order to locate and position the uterus and then forces an instrument into her vagina. The cow is defenseless to stop this violation.*

I am thinking again of Frank, a vegan with whom I, in fact, had three unfortunate encounters. The first time, on Halloween, I cried, and the second time, I bled. The third time, a friend had recently died, and I could not feel my body. I remember the room was cold, and Frank's wife's hair was in the bed, and I lost a bobby pin in the bed, and I felt like my body was meat encased in a thin layer of television static, which a psychoanalyst would later close read as an image symbolizing the period of my childhood when I exclusively watched cartoons about anthropomorphic animals.

After thrice having sex with Frank, I turned into a floating sheet. I felt uncomfortable with the negative emotions I experienced while succumbing to his flesh, not because I did not say no, but because I did not not say no. And in my not not saying no, I did not know how to not say no. So I said *no,* and was not heard, or I was heard but not listened to, and as a consequence, my voice neither was nor wasn't.

To speak the truth, Frank had power over me. He had a wife, and his wife could potentially learn about me. At night, while falling asleep, I would fantasize about her gaining access to my apartment. Maybe a neighbor returning home late would hold the front door open for her; or maybe she would show up in a rage and punch the front door's glass with her fist, and open it, and ascend two flights of stairs. Maybe she would stand in front of my apartment, and knock three times, and I would foolishly answer without looking through the peephole, and there she would be: Frank's wife coming to strangle me. Because I appreciate being choked, I would let her wrap her hands around my neck, and as I would stand outside of myself, I would watch as my eyeballs bulge and my face turns red. "How dare you let Frank enter," Frank's wife would say. *Yes*, I think. *I agree. How dare I?*

Dare I say, I was foolish then. At that time, I thought I was a straight woman. But now I know: I am a gay man. As such, I no longer let straight men enter. Instead, I maintain close proximity to men who have no desire to touch me. Sometimes, it is painful—not because I want these men to touch me, but because there is no one in my life who touches me the way I deserve to be touched; that is, with knowledge of the fact that human beings are animals that need to pet and be pet, hence the expression *heavy petting*, which feels inappropriate in relation to the events I am doing my best to relay here, though I recognize memory is replete with caesuras, and that I am unable to articulate with utmost certainty what exactly happened that night. I made an unwise decision that carved out a space, and in that space, Frank did not think about my body at all, inserting as he did his ego into me: once, twice, three times. In not thinking about my body, he was also not thinking about his wife's body, which is something she points out when she comes over to strangle me: "Now I have a sexually transmitted disease!" And I feel for her, I do. My parent has a sexually transmitted disease, too. When I was five years old, my father said: "I have HIV."

The HIV was contracted during a trip my father took with a man named Dave—his name was Dave, as all men are Dave—a "friend" with whom he was "conducting scholarly research." This trip took place in Florida, where my father and his friend stayed in a hotel with a balcony overlooking a bright blue pool. Do I remember learning how to swim? As my father spoke, I imagined his body slow dancing with his friend. It is night, and it is humid, and as I imagine my father's pleasure, I try to channel how liberating it must have felt to experience—from the Latin *experientia*, from *experiri* meaning *to try*—another man's flesh, as if his skin were meat or one step of the scientific method. I think of my father's sexual encounter with Dave as a learning experience, and I wonder if this moment was filmed so it could be revisited over and over.

Two months ago, I dreamt that a gay man I do not know, whom I met twice through mutual friends, was slow dancing with me in the middle of a cement room. The room was unrecognizable but felt familiar. When familiar yet displaced architectures appear in my dreams, I refer to these spaces as *the [redacted]*. As the gay man I do not know danced with me in *the [redacted]*, I felt treasured, safe. He did not want to take off my pants. He did not place his fingers in my mouth. I knew he would not try to take my integrity away.

As we slow danced, no music played. Nor did I look into his eyes and tell him I loved him. I didn't. Rather, I wanted to *be* him: to possess the ability to sleep with men like himself; men who—for the most part—feel safe, though I realize this generalization about the man's experience of his culture is precisely that, and that my lack of firsthand experience as a gay man—beyond my DNA, my gay DNA—leaves me without evidence to the contrary.

The gay man I do not know places his hands around my waist and holds them there. I close my eyes. I place my cheek on his shoulder. He places his head on mine. The encounter feels close, and this closeness contains an alien quality that brings us even closer. When someone or something is unlike you, you may push it away or get curious about it, violate its boundaries or transgress set expectations in relation to the way you are expected to relate to it. The transgression that takes place between us—myself and the gay man I do not know—is one of the heart. We experience a romantic yearning directed toward one another's souls, the opposite feeling from death. This is also a feeling of gender reversal. For at some point in the dream—when I become bored with dancing, or when the man I do not know takes his head away from mine—I lean down, unzip his pants, and extract his ego from his pale blue boxer briefs. His ego is cold, grey, chafed. I look at it, then place my mouth on it. It does not budge; it does not command its y-axis. Rather, it continues to limply cascade between his legs, and I continue to kneel, trying to rescue it, but in this moment our closeness is dead, though I am very much alive, doomed to replay this encounter for quite some time.

CUT FLOWERS

The monastery's gardener explains that the flowers' centers possess several states. The first is when their centers are flat and yellow, indicating a new bloom. The next is when the blooms' centers are bulbous and blackened, as if blistered and bruised by the sun. This latter state is indicative of the flower's need to be clipped, the gardener says, slicing her forearm with the blade of her hand. Which is why you spent so long trying to cut off your arm.

THE THIRD

There exist two brothers and one lover, but the lover is not shared between the brothers. Rather, the lover is the third; or, one of the brothers is, depending on who is taking the lover's photograph. Often, the subject taking the photograph is the second brother; that is, the brother who is not foremost in the lover's mind, but whose desire to be is visible in every photograph he takes. In every photograph the brother takes of his brother's lover, one can tell the brother wants her.

For example, in this photograph—5×7, high glossy paper, Kodak Portra 400 film, as taken on a Pentax K1000, a 35mm vintage film camera that costs more than the average 35mm vintage film camera due to its relative popularity—his brother's lover is standing behind a tree. Through its branches, light is cast upon her face, which looks like jewelry. (Naturally, men as attractive as the brothers will only accept female accessories whose visages look like glass: the easier to shatter them with, to crack their skulls open with.) (There is no sequitur in the previous sentence, I realize. I got carried away by the sound of her head falling on the floor. Subsequently, I picked up the shards and rearranged them into a distorted portrait, through which I perceive a foreboding sense of self. To reorient your consciousness amidst these sentences' scattered pearls, I shall reiterate that this portrait is not a self-portrait, for a self-portrait is taken by a person who lives alone whereas this photograph was taken by one of the brothers, who live together in an apartment far away from the center of the world.)

It is, simply put, a portrait that conveys one brother's love for his brother's lover—the lover who makes love to his brother. Is this portrait romantic? And whose love, in fact, is it? The shadow begs a question across her face, as does the quality of light: mid-day, bucolic, margarine, honeybee, the interior of a Christmas light—or an egg's yolk. Maybe this lover makes both brothers' hearts flutter. Or maybe she, too, is split in half.

I picture her sitting in the backseat of the brothers' car, holding her lover's—one of the brothers—hand. She does not yet know this brother is a bad listener, because she is young. I know this, however, because I kissed him, and I am old. Let me try to tell you the story without getting too bored. I can't make any promises.

We had had too much to drink while sitting on a blanket, and after we drank and ate olives, dried apricots, and cold clementines, I announced: I need to go home to disassemble my desk. I can help you with that, the lover's brother said. Which is how I consented to getting myself into a situation that resulted not only in the failure to disassemble the desk, but also in my pressing my face against the lover's brother's face, which did not listen to me at all, and instead consumed my mouth.

In Chinese medicine, the tongue is connected to the heart. When one kisses, one therefore licks the heart, not the thoughts. When I kissed the lover's brother, I could not hear him think. I could only speculate that his thoughts were dumb, that they merely grazed the surface of the ocean. Do you want to hear them? I didn't think so. For as I try to imagine myself listening to them, I too tune out and recall, instead, holding the lover's brother's hand in the backseat of the brothers' car as if that moment wasn't happening now but, rather, had happened on a distant night at which I was already looking back from the future. Observe his thumb grazing the acupressure point on my hand connected to the large intestine.

Now I am drinking a warm mug of peppermint tea while trying to trust the chain of thoughts that brought me here. Perhaps I was bored with thinking about the lover's brother's hand. Or perhaps I'm masochistic. For, against my better judgment, once I initially fantasized about him, my body immediately began germinating feelings for the lover's brother, as one might germinate seeds near a heat source following a period of dormancy. The lover's brother was the body that woke me up from a long spell. In this incantation he is a sexual creature, and I am not. But I somehow grew feelings for him, and he deployed me as one might deploy a cup to drink a beverage. And though I did not pronounce my feelings, he could surely feel them at a distance—for all sentient beings are psychically connected to one another, not because of magic, but because all of our bodies are shared. So I wrote him a letter. I had a lovely time, I said. I had a lovely time too, he responded, feigning enthusiasm, as I am feigning distance from myself, and so too from him, by writing this. For if he did not pretend to be warm, I would think him cold in his distance, and if I did not present my experience through feigning distance, one might think I get hot too soon. But it was a hot evening, I think as I finish—a lie I also whisper into the lover's brother's ear as I fall asleep next to his body hoping, for once, that this night won't be the last.

SPORES

I arrive at my acupuncture appointment and say to my acupuncturist: Have you heard of fern spores? My fern spored, I say, and upon noticing it, my skin started crawling, I felt nauseous, and I became so anxious I began to weep. I have also been noticing that when you touch my thoracic spine, it does not feel at peace. It contains a nervous sensitivity, an emotional holding pattern, a deep and primordial grief located just beneath my flesh. Furthermore, as I rest facedown on the table where you press your hand against my back, I notice how your palm grazes the image of what it means to be left.

Did you grow up in a good family, my acupuncturist asks.

Do you mean, was I loved as a child?

Sentences embody an awareness of breath. If the breath is nervous, the sentence shivers. Or, if there is a luminescence in the center of the chest, so too does language glow. To my acupuncturist, I say: I wish I had a jar of bone broth; that would bring me wellbeing in this moment. To which she responds: you own a cookbook replete with instructions for that. And what is *that* beyond a part of speech signifying something previously mentioned? To be alone is not to be alone-alone, the acupuncturist says. Even the trapezius muscles are accompanied by data, and this data functions in collaboration with the muscles, fusing with them, dictating how they behave. In this way, I fused with the fern long before it spored. I unconsciously identified with its asexuality, its chlorophyll, its green, and I began to refer to my flesh as a collection of leaves. So too did I trace my arm's veins, recollecting the vascular. In doing so, I formulated research questions: What tissues in the body conduct water? What tissues flower? If I reduce my crying practice to every other day, will my body reach a maximum threshold of unprocessed liquid, wherein its emotional content transmutes into spores? In other words, if I remain inattentive to my desire—if I avoid it in lieu of watching it, let it grow legs, let it learn to walk on its own, and notice how it walks, where it goes, why it wobbles there, and follow it without judgment or the pretense of an anxious helicopter—will it transmute into breath that knows more than I, and will I in turn come to understand its spores as valentines written to me, granted I am terrified of them, granted they know more than I know?

+

Your hair is very long; I love it, my acupuncturist says. I love touching it, my acupuncturist says, running two hands through my very long hair. But can't I get myself off using a vegetable, I ask. Can't I come alone and feel this chasm in the company of plants? Whereupon my fern spored, I autoerotically induced an emptiness that resulted in my crying in the shower for quite some time. This scene lasted for at least seven minutes. Subsequently, I changed the cat's litter, emptied it into a bag, then tied the bag into a knot. Surely I can get myself off, I think—I with my long hair, I with my very long hair. The climax may not be impressive, but it will provide a window into the everyday experience of being left alone.

+

The spores are the fern's secret, my acupuncturist says. When it spores, the fern is reinventing the world.

+

Like language I deliver to the air, the fern's spores orchestrate a novel, a form of making things new. Imagine: that everything is a technology of writing—from the treadmill's buttons to the fern's spores' lines of asexual propagation, from a metric space sans geodesics to the sound a church organ makes when you sit in a church after a long run, remembering "altar" is a noun, and "to alter" is a verb.

+

I experience a phobic reaction to my fern's spores and move from the side of the room with plants lightly covered in fruit fly-sized bugs to the side of the room containing a purple hanging plant, a succulent that resembles an onion, a small tree, and a spider. I live with aliens, I think to myself. The spider has holes in it. Holes make me shiver, my acupuncturist says. And the tree is a tree my cat always swats in the night, though lately she prefers swatting the pink tropical plant. She knows she is able to wake me by swatting it. Stop swatting it, I say, half-asleep, snapping my fingers. Come here. I pat my chest, indicating I want her to be my sandbag. Sometimes she comes and sleeps. This morning, she wanted to come under the blanket, so I let her. And now I am thinking about how my acupuncturist said an acupuncture blanket induced a cluster of bumps on a patient's skin. The patient was in bed at his parents' house, the acupuncturist said, when his skin began to spore.

Was there a cat in the house, I ask. Maybe the patient was allergic.

As for parents, my acupuncturist and I have four. Mine are divorced, and besides Michelle and Barack Obama, my acupuncturist's are the only couple I can call to mind when I try to call to mind a secure couple. Being in a relationship is hard, the acupuncturist says, and being alone is hard too. You have to take what you can get without settling for scraps.

Here is a photograph of my parents' house, and here is my

father's strawberry shed. My parents' house is covered in plants, and you can see the cottage where I slept if you gaze across the water. I wish I lived closer to them.

Yes, but what is your desire?

My spore-covered fern sits in the window overlooking the tree and the church. At Christmas, the church's digital bells play carols, and these carols carry into spring. Across the street, an identical tree always appears on the verge of collapse. These days, there are hurricanes in the city. I worry. Doom is inevitable. And when I water the fern, I cannot help but recoil at the presence of such perfectly symmetrical furry brown bumps on the backs of its leaves. What are these specimens, I wonder. They look like unprotected sex.

The more I gaze at the fern's spores, the more my skin feels like it's turning inside-out, like the main character in a children's cartoon I ingested as a girl. In it, a second body swings into herself on the playground and becomes an inversion. You can see her vascular parts, as if she is a fern or flowering plant stuffed into a clear plastic backpack containing water and other residual nutrients. Historically, my own skin is temperamental, prone to viral rashes. It reacts to foods including sugar, dairy, soy, and gluten. Once I was allergic to tree nuts, but I am no longer allergic to tree nuts. Now I am afraid of spores.

Thinking the fern's spores are evil, I wipe them away using a napkin and water. They subsequently spread all over the plant, and across the bedroom floor. And to think I annihilated the spores before understanding they were spores, before understanding I too could asexually propagate evil into evil. Now there is a repetitive form in my stomach, and I am doing the deep work by saying this to you. I refuse to tell the truth, but I am evading nothing.

+

A spore is an asexual form of reproduction whereby nonflowering plants may be adapted for survival, often in unfavorable conditions. On the open forum, a stranger writes: *I feel romantic attraction, but sex feels alien to me.* In bed, I lie on my back and look at a lamp in the shape of a breast. On the windowsill, a fern accumulates dust, mealy-bugs, spores. Not all life forms reproduce sexually; Mary was a virgin when she gave birth to Jesus. So states the Bible, and so my mind turns toward Mary as I genuflect upon entering the cathedral. It is a dreary summer afternoon, and the only other stranger in church is genuflecting in front of Mary, too. I am seated in a pew, listening to her weep. As I listen, I consider stained glass and think of parochial school. I resent school, I say to the acupuncturist. It puts students in debt and, like romance, is transactional. A student is graded; a student must arrive to class on time, lest she be punished; a student must attend, or be marked dead. I even had to wear a uniform to school! And it was a site of sexual abuse. Per Mike Kelley's *Educational Complex*, I think about how school buildings strip bodies of desire, as if bodies exist sans genitals.

I was researching asexuality, I say, and I think I may be graysexual.

What do you mean?

I don't desire sex often. Or, at least, I don't desire sex from strangers. I may be generally asexual, but capable of deep sexual desire under certain conditions.

Did anyone touch you when you were a child?

Why do you think you cannot remember?

When you lived with an alien, what did it feel like?

I did not know closeness.

In the cathedral, my reverie renders the stained glass symbolic. In nativity scenes, The Virgin Mary often appears wearing the color navy. Surrounded by a menagerie of men and nonhuman animals, she wears a veil and genuflects in front of the newborn baby Jesus.

Two of the men come bearing frankincense and myrrh, two forms of resin men can bear. Because she is referred to as The Virgin, one might posit Mary as an asexual fern that spored, and Jesus as the offspring of her sporing. One might make this claim so as to avoid a conversation about Mary, age thirteen, being forced to have sex with a much older man, or being raped by a soldier in Galilee, occupied Palestine. One might not want to admit that the color navy Mary wears in nativity scenes is historically inaccurate, and that Mary would have been dressed in a simple peasant's outfit. Mary was poor, and the beads around her neck were made of wood. She was married to Joseph just weeks after she started menstruating. Indeed, one might not want to think about these facts, or have this conversation, because one might desire to avoid conflict, or dislike the feeling of one's systems of belief shattering like glass, or ice, or an actual human heart. Yet it goes without saying: while no nativity scene formally depicts Mary giving birth to Jesus—her violated, naked body exposed amidst the company of men—the shadow of this reality hovers beneath the surface.

I walk from one side of the church to the other.

Aware of my ritualistic performance, I stand in front of five rows of candles and light a burnt match with one candle's flame. The acupuncturist touches my spine, says "Your body is protecting itself." I light another candle, acknowledge the presence of pain, feel substantiated. Is God moving through me? The choir stops singing.

PREACHER

One week before Brett Kavanaugh was nominated to the Supreme Court, I learned that the twenty-five-year-old man who groomed and raped me when I was sixteen is now a preacher who works at a mega-church. When I met him, the preacher was a nontraditional college senior, the lead actor in a community musical theater production of *Joseph and the Amazing Technicolor Dreamcoat*, for which I performed in the wives' chorus. Today, the preacher has three sons, one wife, and a white dog, an image I cannot invoke without calling to mind the phrase "white bitch," which may or may not refer to the preacher's wife, but which does, in fact, refer to me. I am the preacher's unpleasant situation—his living nightmare, even—derived from the Middle English meaning "a female spirit thought to lie upon and suffocate sleepers." And despite the fact of my being a bitch, I had a dream last night wherein a feline bit my finger. Venom surged through my arm as I tried to tear my finger away from her teeth, which left behind a raw, fleshless stump. I woke with five fingers on each hand, and felt surprised I was not bleeding.

The day prior to Brett Kavanaugh's Supreme Court nomination, I drafted numerous private electronic messages to the preacher, the progenitor of patriarchs, none of which I sent. *I feel like I have nowhere to place my rage except this box,* I typed into the corporate social network modeled after high school yearbooks. *Hi! I'm not sure if you remember me,* I typed. *How about this week's headlines?* Then I typed: *I suppose they should come as no surprise. No liberty, no justice, no peace.*

As I studied the photographs of the preacher and his sons on the corporate social network, I telepathically sent him a note. *I hope to God you raise your three sons to have more respect for women than you had when we were acquainted*, I said in my mind, and vividly flashed back to instant messages we exchanged when I was 16. One conversation in particular stood out. It was July 2003, and it was raining, and I was wearing grey leggings, and the temperature in my carpeted bedroom was warm. The preacher—who was not yet a preacher— typed that the weather outside reminded him of sex. I had not yet had sex, so the weather only reminded me of itself. *Why is that*, I asked, to which he responded: *It makes you wet.* Then he asked if I wanted to come over. *Okay, I'll come*, I typed. The preacher lived only a short walk from the yellow prefabricated apartment building where I lived with my single mother. Along the way, I looked up at the trees— bright green, a sign of summer—and felt the vibration of raindrops atop my dollar store umbrella, fuchsia and flimsy and cheap. All the while, I remained cognizant of my feet. There were two of them, as there were two of us, as there would be two ways to remember this afternoon: as my problem, or not. I have never been good at math and am therefore bad at solving equations.

In poetry, the word *caesura* refers to a pause near the middle of a line. Etymologically, the word is derived from the mid-sixteenth century Latin meaning "cut, hewn." I offer this information because, despite being a different medium, a short story is a type of film. Thus, a person can deploy a caesura—a jump cut—wheresoever she wishes; for example, in

       so as to   the memory:

We were in   taking off our   and he

                      and he   on the comforter. I did not

                                snarl, like a

    "no,"

    but *You make me*   ?   *I have to.*

I gripped   tied   gave up   and laughed

    and let him   verb my   neck, my   breast, my

                shoulder. *Please,*

    I said, *don't*   *tell my mother*   She

                          was a

small   against which   the floor   lamp to "masturbate in

front of." I had not   in front   and pressed my

    finger to

and felt

                                lighter

  the car   the box   the handprint   the cigarette   the poster

  the ceiling the bookshelf the nightstand the You are Being

Videotaped   Trespassers will be shot   on-site   smile!

    Danger: submerged objects   the VCR

                            the camcorder

                            the suspension of

                            gravity

Hours after meeting the preacher, I drove to Walmart by myself to stretch my legs and browse cosmetics, but inevitably my sojourn led me into other aisles. At Walmart, I stood in front of a NASCAR poster and felt acutely aware of my vagina. It did not feel how it normally felt. Rather, it burned, and stank, and felt as if someone had placed an object into it without permission. Perhaps this object was akin to a hamburger from a restaurant upon which a chef had spit. Or perhaps it was a dry Q-tip, extracted from a glass jar kept atop a bathroom sink, inserted into someone else's ear, then subsequently discarded into a trash can. Or, the object may have been a leaf from a sturdy houseplant—snake or aloe; jade or pencil cactus—or a permanent marker, a smudge stick, a wooden spoon, the end of a metal stapler, vintage and cold to the touch.

In my paraspinal muscles, I felt an agitated form of disgust, a first cousin to repulsion. Conversely, the NASCAR poster at Walmart depicted an attractive young woman with a white t-shirt pulled up slightly above her chest. Her nipples remained covered, but the bottom portion of her breasts was exposed. The poster measured 24x36 inches, the ideal size for a dormitory wall, and as I looked at it, I began to recite its color palette to myself: blue, red, orange, grey. The woman's skirt's pattern was checkerboard; she wore black sunglasses atop her head. And her hands, albeit static on the poster, kept running through her light blonde hair. *Stop running your hands through your hair,* I thought to myself, and I felt my vagina again, its pubic region covered in razor burn, a direct consequence of shaving. Unlike me, the woman's skin was shiny, and her stomach was toned. Something we shared was the possession of a mouth, often interpreted by strangers as an orifice for gonads. As I studied her mouth, it began to resemble my own, thereby making the poster a surface within which to see myself reflected.

At the bottom right-hand corner of the poster was a barcode, and a proper name: NASCAR Racer Girl Poster Sexy Babe New. She cost $6.99, tax not included.

Amidst the abyssal and unmetabolized rhetoric of the corporate social network—*Men are abusers, I hope they all die; I hope Jill Stein voters kill themselves; neither the Democrats nor the Republicans give a fuck about us; what's the point of anything?*—I did not know what to do about the preacher. Should I write to his church, I wondered, and let them know they subsidize a man who was, at least at one time in his life, a predator? Or should I directly mail a letter to the preacher myself, explaining to him how I thought of him this week, and perhaps signing off with a #MeToo hashtag meant to spook him? Upon considering each option, I settled upon purchasing a postcard for the preacher. The card I chose featured Barbara Kruger's *Your Body Is a Battleground* artwork from 1989, the year I turned three, which just so happened to be the year ACT UP protested the Roman Catholic Archdiocese's public stand against AIDS education and condom distribution at St. Patrick's Cathedral. 111 protestors were arrested that day. My Barbara Kruger postcard cost $1.11, tax not included. It is a known fact that repeating numbers are a sign of angels, so everything felt auspicious, from the postcard—whose photographic silkscreen on vinyl featured a white woman's face split in half, one-half positively exposed in black and white, and the other negatively exposed like a demon, atop which the words *YOUR BODY IS A BATTLEGROUND* were superimposed—to the message I composed on its back: *Thought of you this week. #MeToo.* What would I have written on the back of the NASCAR poster if I could have traveled back in time?

As I navigated the megachurch's website in order to obtain the preacher's mailing address at work, I opted in to viewing a short promotional video about the congregation. The first shot in the video featured a Christian folk group leading a roomful of white people in a praise and worship song. This scene went on for approximately fifteen seconds. In it, the white people held their hands in the air while theatrical lighting illuminated the folk group onstage. This scene was juxtaposed with a brief shot of an empty auditorium, which looked like a movie theater. *We are family*, the video declared. *We are passionate.* Cut to the image of children playing in a room filled with balloons and motivational posters. Cut to the image of a woman wearing a gold cardigan, waving her hands in front of a youth group. Cut to the image of the preacher holding his wedding band-clad hand over the center of his chest, his heart. *We are caring*—the white people jumped up and down, down and up, ecstatically—*we are connected.* Image of a woman in a Pittsburgh Steelers sweatshirt eating salad. Image of a child in face paint gliding down an inflatable slide. Image of a middle-aged man dressed in a Livestrong bracelet being submerged in a dunk tank. *We are world-changers.*

As this evangelical Christian montage played, I muted the video and played "Preacher," a three-minute and forty-four-second indie pop song by Girl Ray, a London-based female trio: *I am your preacher! How did I fall so low? And how am I supposed to let you know?*

As "Preacher" played, the short, muted evangelical Christian montage continued, and I felt a new sort of affective dissonance— giddy anger—induced by the sound of the sugar-coated indie pop song juxtaposed with the megachurch's moving image as I wrote out the preacher's full name on the postcard. I felt as if I were the protagonist in my own video game—Princess Peach in Super Mario World, for instance, who was about to escape Bowser, were she permitted to be the protagonist.

As I copied down the preacher's work address—located just below the megachurch website's embedded promotional video—onto the postcard, I recalled cursive handwriting lessons in Catholic elementary school, a memory accompanied by the cold gaze of Sister Marietta, the eighty–something-year-old nun who told me my lowercase Fs looked too much like Ls, and who led my third-grade class in organized prayer. *Hail Mary, full of grace, who was given no choice but to marry Joseph at the age of fourteen, and to conceive and have his kid,* I recited. Despite her bitter disposition, Sister Marietta possessed warmth, and it was with enthusiasm that I absorbed her analogies comparing cursive letters to rollercoasters. In retrospect, this comparison seems to speak to the experience of Catholic school in general: how it is an amusement park filled with menacing rides and exhibits, bumper cars that crash into one other, a Ferris wheel that makes a person sick, and halls of mirrors that offer distorted representation of children's bodies, wherein to stand in front of a mirror is to accept how the mirror sees you, versus how you see yourself. Catholic school remained on my mind as I walked to the mailbox, sent the postcard, and never heard back.

I am thinking now of the 1987 film *Wings of Desire,* which I saw one afternoon at Film Forum in New York City. That afternoon, I had actually preordered a ticket for Frederick Wiseman's *Monrovia, Indiana*, but when I reached Film Forum, I purchased a ticket for *Wings of Desire* instead. It felt self-indulgent, and I couldn't afford it, but I was attending the film following a psychoanalysis session during which I had articulated something I wanted: to feel free. In the theater, I sat and watched and was enchanted by the film which, despite or perhaps due to its diabolical romanticization of heterosexuality, turned from black-and-white to color.

In one of my favorite scenes in the film, a lonely trapeze artist named Marion sits in front of a three-paneled mirror framed by thick lights. Marion lives alone in West Berlin amidst a caravan of circus performers whose livelihoods are in jeopardy, as their circus group will soon be closing down. It is the night of a full moon, and an angel, Damiel, stands behind the mirror, watching Marion, listening to her thoughts. Despite their proximity, the two are ghosts to one another: Damiel sees Marion, who cannot see him, but can feel him;

and Marion longs for Damiel, who protects himself from being seen. *I have to wake up from this dream*, Marion thinks. In the background, the circus's audience applauds and cheers.

To look in the mirror is to watch yourself think, Marion thinks. *So what are you thinking?* As Marion thinks this, Damiel crouches behind the mirror. Cut to a shot of Marion, looking at herself at us, at which point the camera pans down, concealing her face behind the mirror, until the frame goes black. Then the camera's eyes readjust and look at Marion from Damiel's perspective, gazing at her face not only from behind the mirror, but through it. Across the landscape of the next twenty seconds, the light slowly develops her image until the two exchange a glance.

I think I still have the right to be afraid, she thinks, *but not to talk about it.*

I'm a little bit afraid, she thinks.
It's gone already, she thinks.
All gone, she thinks.
It'll come back.

EMPATHY

We collectively recall standing in front of windows waiting for our father to return. He never did. In this recollection, we are young and alone, and although I cannot picture your childhood home, I can describe mine to you. Picture, if you will, an 8 ½ by 11-inch landscape photograph. In it, I am eight years old and standing in a living room the approximate size of my living room, a living room you've visited and can therefore vividly imagine via the power of your third eye. The dimensions of the past are difficult to discern vis-à-vis the photograph, which is flat, unlike the present, three-dimensional and accented by a jute rug partially concealing its hardwood floor.

The dimensions of the past have no jute rug; the living room in this photograph has its hardwood exposed. I recall getting splinters in my feet from it. I also recall the entertainment system in the center of the room, pressed up against the wall (the color of an egg), and a record player with no speakers attached. In a corner, a record collection exists, about which I recall very little besides the fact that it contained records by Talking Heads, Dire Straits, The Smiths. My parents listened to this music, and so I listened to it too. And now I am thinking about R.E.M., because I loved "Losing My Religion" and would sing it alone to myself to you in the living room.

There was a staircase in the living room, and I would often stand at the top of it and pretend to be a student. I wore a light grey sweatshirt that read *University of Pittsburgh* and carried a backpack, and also wore black leggings and sneakers and my hair in a loose bun. I would often descend the staircase while Pearl Jam's *Ten* played and pretend to flirt with Eddie Vedder, who was invisible to everyone but me. My hair: no one brushed it until it became infested with lice. My mother said the lice meant my hair was clean. But I have no memory of washing it. One memory I do have is of a bathroom where a colony of ants once descended upon a bowl of honey I placed next to a void, a small hole in the wall from which the ants emerged. In this scene, I am naked in the bathtub while my mother announces her father is dead. I am not yet eight years old.

Sometimes, I experience my body as a sheet of paper, and this feeling induces the sensation of slowly disintegrating in water, red ink bleeding out like the menstruating child I am. Red is the color of blood, apples, Santa, and the Republican party. When my period arrived, I was alone in the bathroom, pulling down my underwear. It was December 13, 2000, otherwise known as Doe Day: the day hunters weather snow to slaughter female deer.

Back to our father. He never returned. So tucked away in our collective unconscious is the presence of his absence. As our mother telephoned the cops to ask if dad was dead, we observed her from the hallway adjacent to the den, which is not akin to any room in the apartment I currently inhabit, but is instead its own ethereal world. This may well be for the best. Our first pet, an orange fish named Goldie, died in that hallway. Our father overfed her, an expression that encompasses how the love we give to one another smothers us to death.

Once, I watered a houseplant so many times its leaves turned yellow, then began to fall off, one by one by one.

Once, I told someone I needed him. Shortly thereafter, he left.

Once, a stranger said he needed space. We were entangled in bed, my arms wrapped around him. On the opposite side of the wall, a bathtub spigot was broken. Hot water dripped out from it like a weeping infant.

Once, I typed all of my secrets into an anonymous internet

survey. After I was done typing them, I pressed send. Who, I wonder, was the recipient of my shame?

Once, I tried to love someone whose heart was composed of decay. I convinced myself this love was unconditional, and let him call me names.

I listen to a song about a drunk who tells someone for whom he feels affinity to fuck herself. Then he calls her beautiful. *I get mean when I'm drinking*, he says. *But sometimes I get really sweet.*

I cannot reconcile the tender register of my body fitting into the drunk's with the cruelty of his speech.

In a state, the drunk is playing video games. This practice, he reports, absolves his body of stress.

In the past, my mother is playing *Super Mario World*. Her avatar is Mario—a miniature Italian protagonist dressed in red, with a black mustache, who rides on an imaginary creature named Yoshi, a pseudo-dinosaur that lays eggs. From an aerial perspective, I watch her vanquish demons using only a Super Nintendo console. I observe as she saves the Princess Peach who is being held captive by an evil turtle named Bowser. Bowser hovers in the air in a contraption that resembles a flying car without a hood, and he throws miniature wind-up turtles to Mario, who crushes the turtles and throws them back up into the air, hitting Bowser on the head. Eventually, Bowser retreats. An array of anthropomorphic fireballs descend. Mario dodges them, then Bowser returns. The wind-up turtle sequence repeats until it ends, at which point Bowser's contraption turns over. The Princess, clad in pink, floats down.

Mario's adventure is over, a caption says. *Mario, the Princess, Yoshi, and his friends are going to take a vacation.*

I sit next to my mother on the floor and watch her play *Super Mario World*. I hold one of two Super Nintendo controllers in my palms and press its buttons to mirror the moves my mother makes onscreen. She may be far away, but via this controller, we remain connected.

Tonight, you and I located photographs of our father in my laptop computer. We placed them side-by-side. *Alcoholic*, you said, looking at one. *Workaholic*, I said, looking at another. Then we looked at each other, and our haunted smiles reflected one another in a way that made us feel distanced from our father. This moment comprised a diptych. In it, we were two fictional siblings inhabiting real life.

LOVE LETTERS

CLAIRE (V.O.)

In a dream, I climb a barbed wire razor ribbon fence to touch you. I remove my shoes and socks and scale the metal; fall back, grimace, and redouble. I tear open my legs, arms, and palms to see you on the other side. At the top of the fence, I wave hello. You move your hand to and fro, signaling kinship. And although we cannot speak, it's clear we agree: this screenplay would be easier to write if you weren't you, and I weren't me.

There exists a concrete poem by Louis Aragon entitled "Suicide," which is simply the word "Suicide" followed by all 26 letters of the alphabet. So too exists a poem by bpNichol: *abcdefghijklmNO*. Both of these poets were on the syllabus for my text message crush, Empathy's, Introduction to Creative Writing class, which he taught at a high school in New Mexico the semester we began talking on the phone. Two nights a week at 10:00 p.m. EST (8:00 p.m. MST), we talked about our families, our favorite music, and our mutual obsession with the English alphabet—how, if you look closely, its letterforms resemble playground equipment, minimalist furniture, extraterrestrial plant life, jewelry, weaponry, bones.

Because my text message crush, Empathy, never told me his real name, I fantasized it to be something like *Rolando, Fernando, Olivier, Alejandro,* or *Amadeus.* Honestly, we could have met anywhere. Between our phone calls, we exchanged missives about my dying cat and his dying second wife. Like me, she had thick, black, curly hair, and was preternaturally sensitive. Empathy never told me her specific malady, so I imagined her dying of loneliness or disgust. Why was her husband talking on the phone with a young woman near the Eastern seaboard, and why was he sending this young woman GIFs of letterforms set in seventy-point serif fonts?

O

Empathy and I only spoke via voice chat, so I never saw his face. Only his letterforms, punctuation, and syllabus. Yet our connection was so expansive that, each time we talked, it felt like a key was being inserted into an invisible door that opened out onto a field of letterforms that were draped across grass and hanging from trees, and also rising and falling and hovering, twisting and splitting—and knotting, knotting, knotting, knotting, knotting, knotting.

Empathy signed off his emails *poempathy*—the capacity of a poem to feel another's feelings—which made me think about us trying to feel one another's voices on the phone. He was stuck where he was from, as if in a wind tunnel, and I lived alone in a concrete ATM. We kept each other company. "Are you there?" we would say. "Can you hear me?" During one call, I described a tape journal wherein David Wojnarowicz drives through the desert. "It's funny," Wojnarowicz says in it. "If I try to describe how someone has touched me so deeply, the process of language fails." In this tape journal, Wojnarowicz was driving through Gallup, New Mexico, meditating on isolation; he was somewhere between Albuquerque and Holbrook, traversing land whose monikers are deceptive. On a website, I once read that Albuquerque—originally spelled A, L, B, U, *R*, Q, U, E, R, Q, U E—is haunted by its ghostly *r,* absent due to either a signage typo or a conquistador's revision. But this fact about the letter R—the letter P as a lithe ballerina, stretching out its leg in a *tendu*—may or may not be true.

In spring, I discovered that one of my phantasies of Empathy's name—*Orlando*—when combined with my name, formed a concrete poem in the shape of a circle. This visual puzzle clicking into place made me feel wildly obsessed with Empathy. Via my concrete poem, our names perfectly interlocked, forming a ring of candles that I imagined would burn for all eternity. The word *land*—the middle letters in his sexy imaginary first name—rested at the circle's depression, and *air*—the middle letters in my actual first name—hovered above. The rest of our first names' letters—O, R, and O; C, L, and E—delineated the shape's curved periphery, our enclosure's outer limits. Our letters were fixed above and below one another, but they did not touch. I transcribed the concrete poem using Microsoft Word—"It's important to keep the process as simple and complicated as possible," Empathy joked. We laughed, not because his joke was funny, but because the telephone lines separating our bodies were inherently tragic. Although neither of us communicated this tragedy to the other person

```
              A   I   R
        C L               E
        O R                   O
            L   A   N   D
```

Our concrete poem—our love letters—made me feel insane, as if our connection had been fated across time and space for all eternity. Clearly, Empathy and I were destined to marry one another amidst a field of flowering cacti while food trucks blared new wave songs and served vegan grits, tinned fish, chili raspberry cupcakes, and orange wine in cans. "We are going to write a screenplay," Empathy declared one night. We had been talking on the phone for two and a half hours, and I was sitting on a jute rug in the center of my living room, painting my toenails beige. "It will be about a poet in the desert trying to talk on the phone to another poet in a faraway city, but the signal is poor."

In bed that evening, my brain's merry-go-round circled a speculative screening of our full-length feature film. In one scene, I daydreamed about the former poet driving to a grocery store while listening to Gary Numan, Brian Eno, Devo, The Church. In another, I envisioned the latter poet writing a letter of complaint to T9 Mobile about the dyad's poor cellular connection. *I see we do not have towers in that area,* T9 Mobile would respond, and this response would be shown on-screen in the movie in the form of an automated text message. *In that area, we partner with regional carriers to provide our customers with service.* Via text message, the former poet would also send the latter poet a GIF of a green pepper. It would make the latter poet feel sad but less alone, which a viewer would implicitly understand based on the leading actress's nuanced facial expressions (woeful eyes; pursed lips; a softening of her jaw as she studied the green pepper GIF). After the conversation would die, the poet would cook spaghetti and cry while listening to a couples therapy podcast. Subsequently, one of the poets would start a bonfire, and the other poet—the leading actress—would get stuck in a church parking lot following her attendance at a twelve-step group meeting. This parking lot would be lined with a barbed wire razor ribbon fence atop which a piece of fabric would be stretched. On it would appear a photograph depicting the word *EMPATHY* emblazoned at the peak of a boundary, which would necessarily be the fence that divides San Diego from Tijuana in so-called Friendship Park where, on Saturdays from 10:00 a.m. to 2:00 p.m., people from either side of the border meet to press their fingertips together through thick steel for a maximum of thirty minutes. But why and how would the screenplay shift toward this location?

I once read an essay by French psychoanalyst André Green, who states this claim: *You can be a citizen or you can be stateless, but it is difficult to imagine being a border.* Perhaps, I thought to myself, Green has never experienced his body as a part of the alphabet, as a set of letters in fixed order. Or maybe he has never fallen in love by sending and receiving text messages. "The English alphabet structures what we see without saying it," Empathy says. "The letters of a language constitute a signal, a single human mark." About borders, the philosopher Étienne Balibar writes: "All this, as we know, is not merely theoretical. The violent consequences are felt every day." Adjoining our names, Empathy and I contrive a cusp, an end where two curves meet. In a phantasy, I imagine myself breaking free from the container that gives form to my life in order to enter the circle whose border I am, then study a photograph of a man and a woman looking into one another's eyes. They are covered in Christmas lights and stand face-to-face, but their bodies do not touch. On the printed page, the circumference formed by my name knotted but not knotted with Empathy's creates a margin, blank and empty.

ABCDEFGHIJKLMNOPQRSTUVWXYZ

"We are going to write a screenplay," Empathy repeats. I tell myself this is a sign that we are destined to be together forever. So I write the English alphabet on my forearm in thick black Sharpie, and imagine him doing the same. This correspondence feels so good I want to blow my fucking brains out with a double barrel shotgun.

abcdefghijklmNO

In Friendship Park, the word *EMPATHY*—photographed and framed as a progressive public art installation in one of the most expensive cities in the United States—hovers above the Binational Friendship Garden of Native Plants, a space of civil disobedience comprising three circular gardens, each of which is bisected by the garden's primary barrier, the fence. One garden is a mirror garden, where the same species grows on either side of the wall. The second garden is a garden where all species produce yellow flowers. And the third garden is a cactus and succulent garden where visitors can write wishes on rocks. Running between these circles is a river of sage in the shape of an S, a letterform also equivalent to half of infinity, which is therefore not only a lived critical disarticulation of dominant culture and an act of resistance, but also a concrete poem signifying the finitude of a doomed plot that takes place in four-dimensional reality.

In a notebook, I begin writing an imaginary voiceover for the film I phantasize I will one day co-write with Empathy. The voiceover accompanies a self-reflexive scene inspired by screenwriter Paul Schrader, who throughout his fifty-year oeuvre has depicted and re-depicted very lost men in the act of writing. As in a consummate Schrader movie, the man delivering this voiceover—Empathy—is crouched over a desk, writing in his journal. His handwriting reads:

> *In a dream, I climb a barbed wire razor ribbon fence to touch you. I remove my shoes and socks and scale the metal; fall back, grimace, and redouble. I tear open my legs, arms, and palms to see you on the other side. At the top of the fence, I wave hello. You move your hand to and fro, signaling kinship. And although we cannot speak—the reception is weak, the picture is unclear—we both agree: this screenplay would be easier to write if you weren't you, and I weren't me.*

Crafting this voiceover, I think once more of the French psychoanalyst André Green. To Green, I explain that all plots come to a terminal point, that all sets of letters end. "There is, in fact, a concrete poem by the poet Louis Aragon entitled 'Suicide' which is simply the word 'Suicide' followed by all 26 letters of the alphabet. So too exists a poem by bpNichol: *abcdefghijklmNO*," I say, listening to Green as he writes down my words with his pen.

"You feel disillusioned," Green says. He is skeptical of my position, I intuit, for enclosing one finger on his left hand is a border, a circle, a gold band, a ring: a round plane whose boundary consists of points equidistant from a center. The presence of this O feels meaningful to me, although I choose to not interpret it as a sign, opting instead to transcribe it as a thing.

On November 17, 2018, the United States side of Friendship Park and the Binational Garden was shut down by border patrol. A news report containing thermal camera footage depicts men climbing over the fence, "trying to kick free of damaged razor wire that had just been installed [to reinforce] border security." States a voiceover accompanying news footage: *Just a day before, there were large groups of people at the barrier; some climbing, sitting, even walking on the fence.* Juxtaposed with this sentence is the image of a man walking across the barrier as if it were a balance beam. The fence extends into the Pacific Ocean, whose tides are shown rising and falling via an overhead shot that looks as if it were taken by the moon. As the ocean pulls back, its heat redistributes. *There have been some cases where individuals from the South have thrown objects over on to the North side*—the voiceover, again—and I close my eyes and imagine letters of the alphabet hurtling through space. Nothing can be passed through the fence, Friendship Park's website states; this is a customs violation that includes food, money, gifts, and notes. As the letterforms tumble through the air—the middle letters in my first name, which float above the land—no one is injured, although a portable light gets hit. *Lighght,* I think to myself, reconsidering a concrete poem as a sucker-punched word. Then, to Empathy, I type: *I want to learn more and wonder if there's anything I can do to organize from my*

end. But when I reread this sentence, I see: *I want to learn more and wonder if there's anything I can do to tend.*

After Empathy learned I was writing a screenplay about us—I published a portion of it in a mutual friend's literary journal—he became enraged, and sent me a series of scathing, threatening text messages to which I woke up one Sunday morning. I took half a Klonopin, texted my therapist, and did not respond. I felt ashamed and stupid and young and afraid, and I felt like an idiot for publishing the excerpt from my screenplay, whose likeness mirrored my so-called *real life.* I also felt concerned that Empathy was no longer in love with me, though he had never explicitly communicated that he was. Nevertheless, I understood his love letters bridged the unspeakable. His tirade, however, was not a love letter. Maybe it was a sick form of poetry. In it, he called me a *cuckoo bitch;* he said *fuck you fuck you fuck you;* he said *die hoe corpse;* he said *what gives you the right to write about me, and what gives you the right to write about Friendship Park, which has nothing to do with me?* He also said his dying wife was obsessed with me, and that I could have her. Following that sentence, he added a smiley face emoji—*:)*—that reminded me of the Joker. It was at that moment I imagined holding Empathy's dying second wife on my jute rug while caressing her thick, black, curly hair, and painting her toenails beige. An IV was plugged into her left forearm, and bright red blood flowed into it, as if from a rose. She looked ethereal, so I sang her an original song on acoustic guitar inspired by Sibylle Baier. Then I tilted her head back and poured cool water down her throat to soothe her, and kissed her mouth, after which we floated out the window and circled my house, each other's wives now, knotted together by the unsayable, and a love that could never be writ.

An hour and twenty minutes later, Empathy's dying wife sent me an email. She also called me a *cuckoo bitch*, no smiley face. Reading it, I realized that although I was afraid, I was delighting in having successfully integrated myself into a cyber love triangle, which made me wonder if there might be a flaw in my character. Simultaneously, I also felt bad for harming her, in sickness and in death. In America, everyone is already obsessed with dead women. Case in point: In her email, the dying wife said her husband threw a bowl at her because he was so angry about my romantic comedy.

MY ALBATROSS

I met my Albatross when I was twenty and he was forty-four. "I'm forty-five," he lied, taking a sip from his third double-hopped IPA. In fact, he would only turn forty-five four months later, in July 2007. But in the nine years we spent together, he always preferred to round up. 108 times over the 108 months we were together, I entered my monthly expenses into a spreadsheet while my Albatross commented upon my need to tally cents. "Don't forget to round up," he would whisper, wrapping his arms around me from behind, kissing the top of my ear, placing his chin on my shoulder, breathing down my neck. In these moments, I imagined we were a pair of birds, my Albatross and I, monogamous for life. But monogamy was his burden, my Albatross, and he made his burden my own. Instead of a cross, my Albatross about my neck was hung.

We met in mid-May, at a dive bar called Cookie's in Pittsburgh, PA. Cookie's was owned by a married couple, Jennifer and Steve, a pair of tall and tattooed ethically non-monogamous birds. Jennifer and Steve dated strangers of every gender—men and women with color-ful tattoos of varying degrees of quality; non-binary tango dancers; genderfluid children's librarians, beer-makers and sommeliers; and androgyne angels whose faces impressed themselves upon the mind like mantras. In 2007, one year before Barack Obama was elected president, this wide spectrum of genders was a hard pill to swallow for consumers and mainstream culture. University instructors did not yet ask students for their pronouns, nor did dating apps repre-sent genders outside the binary. I identified as a woman, resented the word "female," used the pronouns *she, her, and hers*, and dated everyone, which made me pansexual, a term I did not know at the time that now reminds me of a détourned Williams Sonoma that sells expensive vibrators alongside Le Creuset crockpots. And although cell phone-based dating apps did not yet exist in 2007, I imagine if they had, I would have downloaded one and swiped until I reached a photograph of Jennifer and Steve's half-naked torsos, accented by rope knotted per Japanese shibari, which would have been attached to their combined profile articulating something about a unicorn, a mythical animal represented as a horse with a single, straight horn. *Seeking a unicorn*: upon encountering this phrase, I would have asked myself whether I wanted to be second, third, or neither, and then I would have swiped to the left or the right depending upon the potency of my ambivalence.

Following the 2008 election, Jennifer and Steve found themselves thrice doxxed by white supremacists. On the most notable occasion, a SWAT team was sent to Cookie's, purportedly by a group of local neo-Nazi teenagers who read about the bar's faux-dive ethos in a news article posted on 4chan. Why neo-Nazi teenagers would dox left-leaning bar owners in Pittsburgh felt beyond me at the time, even when the situation's facts were outlined in the *Post-Gazette:* "The teenagers sought to recruit countercultural sympathizers; simultaneously, they wished to drive Cookie's out of its historically conservative neighborhood, Morningside."

Anyone can participate in white supremacy, regardless of one's cultural signifiers, but the idea of a neo-Nazi valuing Cookie's strings of multicolored Christmas lights, its My Bloody Valentine poster, *E.T.* projected on a brick wall via light, Sibylle Baier's *Colour Green* and The Coup's *Pick a Bigger Weapon* and Spacemen 3's *Recurring* on the jukebox—seemed unlikely. "Set me free," my Albatross would sing along with Spacemen 3 while settling his tab. "Baby, I got the key." His voice was a deep baritone, and in our nine years together, I loved to overhear him singing in the shower, in the car, and over french fries in shared booths, wherein his voice always called to mind a description I once read of the albatross: that it is the most legendary of all birds, an oceanic creature with a wingspan at times greater than ten feet.

My Albatross was not particularly attractive, and thus not worth describing in great detail. He stood at approximately five feet, ten inches, the height of an average male. He did not possess clear skin, a flaw that reminded me of my dead crush, Arthur Russell. Nor did he possess a penis the length of a wine bottle. Rather, my Albatross's penis was merely okay—not the sort that warrants surgical enhancement, nor the kind that does not fit into a regular condom—and his other attributes were okay too, as evidenced by the fact that, on his forty-fifth birthday, a stranger on the most popular corporate social network that existed at the time remarked upon his big, bright smile, and his eyes the color of celestine, a mineral purported to help sleepers swim to the depths of their unconscious in order to lucidly dream.

In the glow of this compliment, my Albatross and I purchased a chunk of celestine at a New Age gift shop in San Francisco, which we visited while on a cross-country road trip dedicated to record digging, the practice of seeking out records that everyone else on Earth has abandoned or sold. "Which mineral resonates at the level of your soul," I asked him as we stood in front of black tourmaline, blue agate, rose quartz, aventurine. "I don't believe in souls," he said. "But I appreciate how celestine reflects the color of the sky."

We purchased the mineral, and subsequently walked to Amoeba Records, where we spent three hundred fifty dollars on goth rarities, along with a mislabeled first pressing of Judee Sill's *Heart Food*, a record from 1973 that she wrote, arranged, and produced herself, released to acclaim but few sales. According to the free encyclopedia, the record's lyrics bear the hallmarks of Sill's interest in the occult and Christian theology. The record's last track, "The Donor," contains a choral arrangement in tandem with chants of "Kyrie Eleison":

Lord, have mercy; Lord, have mercy. "This record should cost at least sixty dollars," my Albatross said, and my mind turned to how, when listening to "The Donor" for the first time as a college junior, seated behind the desk at the antiquarian bookshop where I worked for three dollars more than minimum wage, the song lifted me out of my body, alleviated my burdens, made me undead—*Lord, have mercy*—for in the weeks leading up to hearing "The Donor," I ritualistically carved my flesh with X-Acto knife blades procured at the art supply store across the street from the bookshop. This independently owned shop marketed its goods to art students from Carnegie Mellon, a nearby university that offered excellent albeit extravagantly priced architecture and fine arts programs. As I selected a pack of blades from a wall lined with razors, I foolishly imagined myself to be the first creative writing undergraduate in the history of Pittsburgh to ever make such a purchase.

Standing by a wall of hardcover first editions preserved in plastic dust jackets—*The Crying of Lot 49*, *The Recognitions*, *Dhalgren*, *The Virgin Suicides*—I pressed the X-Acto blades to the fleshiest part of my forearm, lightly at first, then scraped the surface enough so the top layer of my flesh rubbed off like dust, after which I dug in a little more. There was some blood, but not too much. As I experimented with the blade, I felt dramatic and in control, and prayed for scars of any size: small, medium, large, extra. Years later, I would learn on a podcast that my carving practice was linked to my need to assuage pain, and to make reality feel more real, and that my desire for strangers to see these scars was linked to my need for someone to bear witness to my suffering, which would, in turn, grant me permission to keep carving. As I carved, I pictured my body as naked as a turkey—a pristine chest and stomach and legs in stark juxtaposition to two arms, covered in oceanic birds with narrow wings, frustration, guilt, blood, sorrow.

Sometimes, I hit myself and allowed my flesh to make a cracking sound against itself; sometimes, I hit so hard my nails would scratch my flesh. Hitting guaranteed a different sort of bruise—purple like an amethyst, with specks of black blood rising to the surface, and pronounced veins. As the bruises faded, they turned puce: dark red, purple-brown, the color of a flea. Because I rarely vomit, this hue felt novel, as if my body were purging itself of itself, extracting its own interior and imbuing it atop the surface of my flesh, branding me like a cow.

As my X-Acto knife ritual became routine, I began purchasing oversized vintage sweaters to wear to class—cardigans and cable-knits, checkerboards and florals, solids and stripes and paisley—though I liked my collection of cuts and bruises and wanted to display them for the entire world to see. I imagined they marked me as dangerous—a creature who bites—and at the gym I reveled in exercising next to oversized men while wearing tank tops that exposed my marks. But covering them made me feel like I was keeping a secret, obfuscating my Albatross, and I also liked the sensation of hiding. It made me feel like I was covering my face with a paper plate to evade a turtle fearfully retracting into its own shell. As dead psychoanalyst D.W. Winnicott once wrote, "It is a joy to be hidden, but disaster not to be found."

In San Luis Obispo, our midpoint destination en route from San Francisco to Los Angeles, my Albatross and I slept with the sky blue celestine mineral on our nightstand as we entangled in one another's embrace like coral. Our hotel, a big box whose name I cannot recall, was located across a parking lot from the Madonna Inn, where we drank red wine while unwrapping the celestine from a gift box containing a slip of paper articulating the mineral's metaphysical properties. *Celestine: Cosmic Lullaby,* its title read, followed by a paragraph: "The celestine crystal inspires deep relaxation by restoring your natural state of joy. Keep a stone in the bedroom and bring tranquility and harmony into your space, the perfect medicine for a restful sleep."

In bed, my Albatross pressed the celestine to my third eye, then ran his thumb and index finger across the lace band of my underwear—below the small of my back but above my tailbone—against which he paused to press his thumbnail, inducing magnetism. I kissed him on the chin, bit his neck.

"What are you doing," I said.

"Initiating a sex scene," my Albatross said.

My Albatross was always intervening with my narratives, imagining himself at their center, projecting himself into characters who consumed one another, when the truth of the matter at the time was that I imagined all living men to be too boring to inspire fiction. Instead, they were accessories—mise-en-scène comprising the various events that made my life—whereas the fictional men I composed were permutations of my darkest, innermost recesses: secrets I would not share with anyone; black boxes tucked away and preserved for the sake of privacy.

"Don't be a bad boyfriend," I said to my Albatross, then licked his cheek, then lightly slapped it. "Write your own short story."

I never used to be one of those women—by which I mean, one of those women who says, *All men are like this*—but somewhere in the middle of my relationship with my Albratoss, I became one of them. "All men are predators!" I remember screaming aloud during a particularly turbulent fight. My Albatross had pissed me off by making up a lie related to the night we met. 18-year-olds are adults, he explained to me, explaining away the fact he was a predator. "So? I was twenty when you met me. Technically, I was still in the developmental stages of my youth. When I was a fetus, you were twenty-four. When I was fourteen, you were thirty-eight. Our relationship can be considered through the lens of statutory rape."

One sunny afternoon, in the middle of a public park, I found myself drunk and telling off my Albatross. "All men are rapists!" I screamed. On this occasion, my Albatross had recently abandoned me for someone else. He had treated me like shit that week—commissioning me to perform little chores for him: Will you read my book review? Can you cook dinner while I meet Dave and Steve? Do you mind washing my clothes? As I performed these tasks, my Albatross had sex with a second body. And after he had sex with it, he came home and held me, a closeness that felt safe. Sometimes while we held each other, we had sex, and when we did, the sex felt lifeless, dull. I felt close and far away; I felt resentful at being one body out of several; I saw our breakup coming but could not accept it when it did. And unfortunately for me, our breakup was only temporary. We got back together within the span of two weeks, during which I watched all of *Twin Peaks*, seasons one and two, and fantasized about fucking Agent Cooper. We would hang upside-down together, blood draining from our feet into our genitals, and after we were done hanging, he would take me from behind on the cold wood floor. "All men are rapists," I screamed at Agent Cooper too. To which he calmly responded: "Not all men are evil."

During those two weeks, I couldn't stop thinking about *Twin Peaks*. I thought about mirrors. I thought about Bob. I thought about Leland, the Possessed. I thought about Maddy Ferguson. And I thought about a particular episode's mise-en-scène: an afghan, a beige couch, a turntable, lace curtains, a white horse. A record spins, emitting no music. In a bathroom mirror, the Possessed gazes at himself. His hair is bright white in one dimension, dark grey in another. His eyes are sky blue; he smiles with teeth. His ghost makes an ugly sound. Laughs. Sound of thunder. Yellow wall. Then the Possessed reaches into his coat and removes a latex glove. Places it on his right hand. Reaches into his coat and removes another. Places it onto his left. Cut to Maddy descending the stairs. Sarah, the Possessed's wife, is lying at the foot of the stairs. There is a wedding ring on her finger. Maddy screams. The Possessed runs toward her: strangles her, beats her, slow-dances with her. He is and is not himself. Sarah remains on the floor, still and unresponsive. Her wedding ring is an object in the shape of an O. O, Maddy on the couch, youthful and screaming. O, how the Possessed punches her. O, how the Possessed dances with her. *Laura,* he says. *My baby.* Kisses her chin, her neck. Then smashes her face into a poster that says Missoula, Montana. After which he holds her.

A friend taking a class on how to cultivate healthier relationships says my proclivity to call all men this or that is a reflection of my rage, and that this rage is being physically absorbed into my bones like calcium, giving me strength. My friend says she's proud of me, and of my rage, which feeds my legs, and I can't help but picture myself standing on two feet in the center of a beach, where I look up at the sky—the pale blue, celestite-colored sky. Above me, my Albatross hovers, glides, then descends into a dream.

Dream-content: I am walking on my hands toward *Moonbird*, a sculpture by the artist Joan Miró. I do not know this sculpture is *Moonbird*, the most prominent element of the dream, but I know. Somehow, I know. The sky is colored between red and white, as in a salmon fish.

    Walking upside-down on my hands, I approach *Moonbird*, who looks like *Moonbird* looks: bulbous, jet-black, and low to the ground. Its face is a crescent moon, and a pointed horn protrudes from the center of its head. I think, *Moonbird is peculiarly lunar,* by which I mean, *Moonbird* is strange in the dream.

    A figure is seated atop *Moonbird*, its groin pressed into the sculpture's horn. The figure's legs dangle over the horn, only they do not stop where my mind normally perceives a pair of legs to stop. Rather, the figure's legs dangle down and coil around *Moonbird*'s curved shapes, much like how a snake coils around a person's legs, arranging itself in a spiral chain of rings. I look up at the figure and wave, moving my feet to and fro, wiggling all ten of my toes.

The figure waves, then disappears.

"Moonbird," I say.

Moonbird looks at me.

"Open your palm," *Moonbird* says.

I look down at my palm. In the middle of it rests a small, pink tablet, smaller than my smallest fingernail.

"Swallow it."

I touch the tablet to make sure it's real. I hold it between my thumb and index finger. I hold it up under my nose. It smells like nothing. I brush the tablet against my lips. I lick it. It tastes like beer. Aware that *Moonbird* is watching, I place the tablet on my tongue. I hold it in my mouth and taste its flavor. Once the flavor disappears, I swallow it. My throat feels cold. I place one hand over it. I gag for breath. Desire, I conclude, is all in my head. I squeeze my neck, furthering the constriction. The landscape turns the color of pink blossoms.

"Moonbird!" I shout.

"What?" *Moonbird* says.

"I love you," I say.

Moonbird screams.

On the night before my Albatross moved out of our apartment for good, I packed his objects. As I packed them, I hated them, and consequently hated him for taking them and leaving me. There were two pairs of gym shorts, empty pharmaceutical bottles, French language dictionaries, matchbooks, used records, an unopened packet of tools for brushing our cat's teeth, and a box of organic condoms. Eventually, I began to unpack a large maroon trunk where my Albatross kept his socks. Most of my Albatross's socks were thick—one pair was made of wool and embroidered with sheep; another pair was emblazoned with a bright blue checkmark. Located amidst the thick socks were a thinner pair of socks, small, balled together into the size of a fist. These socks were a pair of tiny black socks my Albatross bought to wear underneath his slip-on shoes, checkerboard patterned and evocative of Southern California. I remember he bought these tiny black socks because he did not want his shoes to stink, but ultimately grew to love them as aesthetic objects. "When I wear them, I feel like a ballerina," he said.

And so it is with melancholy and remorse that I possess one highly specific memory of my Albatross during the last days of our domestic partnership. When my mind turns toward this memory, all registers of disdain fall away, and I feel my heart, my thoracic cavity, alight in my chest like a log. In this memory, my Albatross is wearing his tiny black socks in our shared bedroom. He is standing in front of our record collection—punctuated by Alice Coltrane and Karen Dalton—trying to get my attention. "Hey," he says. "Look at me."

And without further ado, my Albatross stands up on his tiptoes and smiles, and performs a little dance meant to delight and entertain. Like a ballerina, he raises his arms above his head, and I, sitting in the center of our bed, watch him and laugh. He prances across the room, performing an allegro; he pauses and pirouettes, takes a beat, then assumes fifth position. "I didn't know your legs could do that," I said—after which he lifts one leg, followed by the next, then raises his right arm above his head and bows.

And thus his grand finale punctuates our ending. After his ballet is through, my Albatross sits on the edge of the bed, fingers the chunk of celestite on our nightstand, picks it up, presses it to my third eye, then looks into my two eyes, and bites my cheek. I bite back, and we entangle our limbs on the bed, until there passes a weary time, and each of our throats is parched, and each eye grows glazed until our souls fly from our bodies, and we are left alone.

BONE PIECE

There are bones around which I desire to wrap these words, as if language is a bandage. The bones beneath language are a framework: they support its body but are not the body itself. Nor is language itself a body. Rather, it is a skin. Language's body, after all, is only activated when words are processed by the mind. And then the body fades—so it flickers in and out of being, like these words flicker on and off the screen as I type. Its form is none other than emptiness, per the Heart Sūtra. And *heart* is an anagram for *earth*.

It is a mistake, I think, to assume letters themselves are bones. But they do, in fact, contain bones, and these bones are referred to as *typeface anatomy.*

The dictionary reminds me that *bone* as a verb means "to study a subject intensively, often in preparation for something"—as in, *boning* up on language. In the United States, this verb is also vulgar slang for a man fucking someone. This image cuts close to the bone; it penetrates my mind; I experience discomfort at the hand of the image. Perhaps this is because the image reminds me of fucking a man at a long wooden table. We have been eating fish while arguing about the correct ways to speak to one another. *I have a bone to pick*, he says but does not say. And I feel it in mine, it cuts to the, I make no but throw a—a thing made of, or once made of, such a substance; for example, a pair of dice.

A depression or hollow in a bone is called a *fossa,* whereas a *fovea* refers to a small pit at the head of a bone. A cursory internet search for *fossa* covers my computer screen in images of a catlike mammal endemic to Madagascar. I look into its eyes, then navigate toward a page about planetary nomenclature, and learn that even extraterrestrial bodies such as the moon contain depressions.

Sometimes, pit craters form on the moon. They are naturally occurring voids that result from troughs stretching and breaking due to the weight of nearby volcanoes.

Bearing in mind the future colonization of Mars, I read, we must keep in mind the locations and formation mechanisms of its depressions.

To think of depression as an alien phenomenon, a sunken place.

Because letters are bones covered in ink, language itself is composed of skeletons.

/

Here I could write the history of the first letterpress (Gutenberg circa 1500), or I could write about Chinese woodblock printing (circa AD 175), used to circulate the message of Buddhism, of emptiness, of form's hollow. The combined form of these processes is also known as relief printing, and is considered the earliest form of printed language in the world. Ink, paper, and pressure combine to inscribe language, leaving a depression in paper. Which begs the question: who is depressed? Language or paper?

I am a sheet of paper, meaning I was once a tree. Then someone killed me.

GRAVITY AND GRACE, THE CHICKEN AND THE EGG, OR: HOW TO COOK EVERYTHING VEGETARIAN

for Ian Hatcher

There are many ways to love a vegetable. The most sensible way to love it is well-treated.

M.F.K. Fisher, *How to Cook a Wolf*

That's what I don't understand. Why does one say, "I love you"? Do you understand? Why can't one say, for example, "Egg"?

Daisies, dir. Věra Chytilová

The egg would not become rectangular and anyone struggling to make it rectangular would be in danger of losing his own life.

Clarice Lispector (tr. Giovanni Pontiero), "The Egg and the Chicken"

PREFACE

Into the camera, my platonic friend Ian Hatcher *[he is gay; we do not touch]* holds up a long bean containing three pods. I hold up a piece of popcorn. Our two-dimensional, moving image temporarily induces the laughter god knows we need. What creature do you see? I ask, rotating the popcorn 360 degrees. A face distinguished by the sky's clear moon? A shadow framed by its history? A chicken whose features resemble a dinosaur's? Maybe your popcorn came from the sea; I think I see a turtle in it. And possibly a runaway rabbit. It's the year of the pandemic. Will it ever end? Ian Hatcher walks through a garden in the Pacific Northwest while I lie in bed in a shitty metropolis. We're alone together, bound by screens, although I don't know what my body projects. So I focus my attention upon it like I'm watching a black-and-white movie. Nor could I anticipate this lifelong collaboration with pain, one or both of us says—but also transcendence. Look! There is a bee on my finger, and I am sitting across from you, and you are touching the bee with your finger.

How are you envisioning this?
Via direct experience.
And what are you experiencing now?
That nothing becomes what we think.

On <u>PsychCentral.com</u>, she takes an eighteen-question automated online quiz to help determine if she should see a mental health professional for the diagnosis and treatment of depression. She scores a fifty-four, indicating she is *severely depressed*. Is this before or after she cooks the meal consisting of an orange carrot (unpeeled, cut in circles), red potatoes (unpeeled, thinly sliced), purple cauliflower (a deep violet color), cannellini beans (organic, canned, non-BPA lined), green kale (bunched with rubber), garlic (hardneck), and garlic scapes (whose shapes resemble jewelry)? She imbues herbs and spices: basil, cumin, dill, mustard seeds, parsley, thyme, salt, and pepper. She boils a pot of water, places an egg in it. Clarice Lispector: *The egg is the chicken's great sacrifice. The egg is the cross the chicken bears in life.* In the end, the egg—like love—cannot possibly exist. But, like love, it does, possessing nothing.

For three minutes, the egg boils. Then she removes it from the water with a ladle, ladles it into a bowl filled with water and ice. She lets it cool. Peels off its shell. Atop a second bowl, she pierces the undercooked white in its center with her finger. Is this what it means to destroy an object? Now the egg is vanquished.

Cognizant she is performing a violent act, she penetrates the egg's yolk, watches as it breaks open and spills. While the yolk separates and pours away from its white, she mourns the egg as she mourns her life before and after the virus, the split between her and her friends, the gym where she would try to regulate her moods, and the food coop where she would work and retrieve quality ingredients for omelets. The food coop is now staffed by essential workers instead of by volunteers, introducing a divide between those operating the checkout register and those nervously procuring groceries. Holding the egg, her heart, she hums the song by the band The Sundays whose lyrics are *desire's a terrible thing / it makes the world go blind*, and mourns her country, a clear liquid from which she too feels divided. [*Love is also the deception of what one believed to be love.*]

Excluding love, the list of her desires is as follows: fog, the ocean, a laptop computer, a vegetable garden, a brood of backyard chickens, a bonsai tree, bunk beds, a bicycle, to communicate with clarity and intention, to be scratched on a bench in a cemetery, to better understand the incongruences between people that punctuate everyday life, and a hug. [*This does not make an honorable exception of love.*] If she waits long enough, these desires float away into the imagination that fills the void, where she could go on breaking yolks—attaching her desires to concepts and objects, thereby murdering them—but her attention span is short; she can barely read. To this notion, she holds on for a beat, thereby strengthening a sense of distraction.

On the table, the mint green bowl emits steam. Its color invokes a hospital's walls, a mental institution, a prison. In accordance, she types "stagnation" into the rectangle she uses to escape the world, but it's too late: the sacrifice was made; the killing has occurred. The egg is broken. And, as with all the worst things that change us, love persists as a sign of the egg's fracture.

In dedication to her platonic friend Ian Hatcher, she prepares a pot of quinoa seasoned with yellow curry. What are you making, he asks, astride time and space. She lists the meal's components: chickpeas (organic, canned, non-BPA lined), lacinato kale (chopped into ribbons), an orange carrot (unpeeled, cut in circles), and garlic scapes (whose shapes resemble jewelry). As the kale steams, she juliennes basil and trims a chive blossom until its amethyst petals cascade across the counter, invoking a light onion aroma.

In the screen, Ian Hatcher is inventing a new language to make eggs float above imaginary planes. His language is a language that exists atop an old one, the function of which is to express the relationship between things, e.g., *an egg floats in space as two whales float in space*; or, *a tree is grounded—so too is a house.*

The tree's leaves are red. One whale is dead. And "a mind enclosed in language is in prison," Simone Weil says.

A work of architecture, the quinoa sits under the kale under the chickpeas under the carrots under the julienned basil under the amethyst chive blossom petals under a pinch of chili flakes. Her architecture is sited in the mint green bowl; in the Pacific Northwest, Ian Hatcher eats from a grey bowl the color of a thunderstorm. At her bowl's periphery rest three strawberries whose stems extend far beyond the screen's frame. Ian Hatcher takes a screenshot. In an instant, he will alter the photograph's size and upload it to the cloud. To do so will be to detach the mind from language, to smear the berries onto conceptual boulders, and to wait.

It is minutes before midnight on the day of the incessant birdsong and sirens outside her bedroom window, a metaphor for the alternative novel universe year she is taking one day at a time. So too is this the day her landlord enters her apartment without consent. In bed, she is trying to narrow the distance between herself and the computer—to show it she wants to be near it, to make it realize how special it is to her, to get it to love her back. Before her landlord knocks, he enters. On-screen, Ian Hatcher types: *Are you sure you aren't the same as you once were?*

In the kitchen, her landlord studies the stove's ignition. It burns blue but won't stop sparking.

In a separate message, Ian Hatcher types: *A hen in my parent's coop has been killed by a fox.*

She pictures a fox hunting under the cover of darkness, tearing open a rabbit wire fence surrounding a brood of chickens with its teeth, gaining entrance, then grabbing a hen in its mouth and tearing it apart like tissue paper. The fox licks its lips, swallows the hen's feathers [*she who thought her feathers were to cover her precious skin*]. Covered in its own blood, the hen is white and red. Now the hen is dead. There's something erotic about it. The thought turns her on, and against her better judgment, she texts this to Ian Hatcher.

She uses the sharpest knife to cut base ingredients—purple scallions (a deep violet color), ginger (the rhizome of a plant), garlic (hardneck), garlic scapes (whose shapes resemble jewelry). She heats the base ingredients in sesame oil, covers them in salt and pepper. As they heat in metal, the kitchen heats, and the wooden spoon that rests atop the pan heats. And she too grows heated. Concurrently, she fills a measuring cup with water, removes a container of miso from the refrigerator. Using the sharpest knife, she slices two leaves of green kale (organic, bunched with rubber), taking special care to carve away the spine.

She is tired but takes care of the soup. She pours in two cups of water and stirs. She adds the kale and a tablespoon of tamari, a pinch of chili flakes, a cluster of bean thread noodles. When the soup is cooked, she pours it into the mint green bowl the color of a hospital's walls, a mental institution, a prison. The bowl emits steam. Atop it, she gently places three edible yellow flowers, and recalls a quotation from Simone Weil: *It is the innocent victim that can feel hell.*

Memory-content: Once upon a time, she lived a life as a hen in a coop with eight other hens in upstate New York. Her days were spent picking at grass, looking under trees for worms, and dust bathing. She loved to forage then, and hoped her foraging would one day make her a rare bird—one in a thousand—so that her body would release a double egg that would, in turn, yield a double yolk.

When she was a hen, a fox took her in his mouth, tore her apart. "He's terrible," another hen laughed [*and shrugged it off*] before the tearing took place. Every day, she thinks: how could another creature laugh like this? And what exactly is a hen to do to protect another hen from a fox?

First, the fox was surprised she was [*redacted*]. "Are you sure?" the fox said. "Of course I'm sure," she said. "You make me [*redacted*]," the fox said. (Ironically, the fox was plant-based.) Each time she carves vegetables, she thinks of the fox, of how he said: "[*redacted*]," a sentence she repeats in her head every day. Only once did she repeat it outside of her head. She was eating dinner with a friend. They were exchanging rape narratives over miso risotto. Then they were crying on a log beside a lake. Then they were walking up a hill, exchanging necklaces. Have you seen *Claire's Knee*, her friend asked. No, I haven't. Is it a film about rape?

Taking special care to carve away the kale's spine, she admires the sharpest knife, how its metal reflects the light in juxtaposition to her life's dark spots. She imagines the horror of doing harm to the fox—stabbing it, gutting it, digging a grave for it, burying it. In her mind, she has murdered it so many times; all she wants to do now is forgive. It follows, perhaps, that she is as fearful of the knife as she is reverent. When she is done carving, she immediately runs the instrument under water, and hangs it over the stove on the magnetic strip where other knives reside. If she forgives, she is an apologist; if she doesn't, she is forever a hen. The tension between these ways of being in the world is directed both vertically and horizontally, and it remains unclear which direction to choose. To reconcile herself, she returns to bed, where she will sleep for hours and dream of being dead.

On Father's Day, she composes a salad from mixed greens (resembling a field), avocado (green butter), almonds (roasted and salted), an orange carrot (unpeeled, cut in circles), blackberries (a deep sapphire color), and peaches (grown in South Carolina). For balance, she adds edible nasturtiums (red and yellow), and the juice of one lemon (squeezed by hand). It is a June night mere hours before the Full Strawberry Moon, whose moniker references the time of year when berries ripen. It is in the sky, clear and visible. Time is passing, but it will be many years before her father's soul exits his body. This is her worst fault: to think of death in lieu of aliveness, to speculate the future as it haunts the present. She sits down at the kitchen table with her computer and her dinner, and she stares into the mint green bowl the color of a lace dress, a bread box, a Lucite link necklace. She pierces the salad's leaves, looks down at the computer's keys. She types *Happy Father's Day to the first vegetarian I knew* and sends it to no one—not even her own father—and imagines covering her computer in hen meat.

She wakes up and decides to make buckwheat and coconut flour pancakes, blended with coconut milk and blueberries. Mixed by hand, they are the product of a recipe she learned from the singer-bassist she befriended while traveling with Ian Hatcher through Portland, Maine, many years ago. She has not talked to the singer-bassist since then. Their friendship became a relationship that ended in screaming. It feels like a form of reclamation to cook a recipe that connects her to someone with whom she is no longer on speaking terms. As a mantra, she repeats to herself: *Reclaim the pancake.*

The pancakes have a certain veggie burger aspect to them, which is disappointing and makes her feel alone. The red blob at the peak of their y-axis is homemade strawberry-rhubarb compote, which she made last night. When she cuts into one of the pancakes, it somehow remains uncooked and spews liquid. She takes a photograph, alters its dimensions, and sends it to Ian Hatcher. *I tried to make the buckwheat pancakes again,* she types. *They always end up so fucked.*

To which Ian Hatcher responds: *Have you ever tried using blue corn flour in the mix?*

In Portland, the singer-bassist formed a dozen of these buckwheat and coconut pancakes for her and Ian Hatcher. Topped with raspberries and maple syrup, she remembers the pancakes were juxtaposed on a plate with chilled slices of seedless watermelon. What colors were the plates? And how do seedless watermelons become seedless? On that same trip to Portland, she drank a substantial amount of apple cider vinegar and met a brood of backyard chickens. At night, she slept next to Ian Hatcher [*he is gay; they do not touch*], who later typed: *Are you sure you aren't the same as you once were?* As he slept, she thought to herself: *Am I sure we aren't the same?* His sleeping sounded like a soft, warm glitch. The sunroom where they slept was lined with oversized French windows overlooking a vegetable garden. In the morning, they awoke and discussed the ancient tuxedo cat who did or did not enter the room. As they spoke, she thought of their bed as a boat: how they were out at sea together, safely stowed away. As the morning progressed, the sunroom became warm.

Weeks prior, Tim Hecker—whose songs sound like musical ink-blots—slept in the same bed. Tim Hecker slept until two p.m., the singer-bassist said. Three weeks later, she stood in the middle of a ballroom Tim Hecker transformed into a cathedral. Bright green and pink lights flooded the space, conjuring Earth's folds. In Maine, the bed where she and Ian Hatcher slept was partially made. Did Tim Hecker leave it this way, thereby impressing a trace? To sleep with a stranger's trace may be akin to sharing a bed with a ghost. And to sleep with a ghost sounds more tantalizing than sleeping with a musician or eating shitty, half-cooked buckwheat pancakes inspired by a former paramour. But here she is, masturbating alone during the pandemic with her fancy new vibrator while listening to Tim Hecker's *Haunt Me, Haunt Me Do It Again*.

A computer is not a stranger; it is a familiar object one knows. At home, she continues to narrow the distance between herself and it—to show it she wants to be near it, to make it realize how special it is to her, to get it to love her back. At night, she sleeps with it at the foot of her bed, where its small light pulsates in rhythm with her breath, and where the light's illumination casts a glow against the darkness. In the morning, she opens the computer—feeds it, recharges it. She presses its keys, thereby entering her consciousness into it in order to more deeply fall. Does the computer love her too? From the way it sits like an illuminated manuscript atop her mint green desk [*a prison*], it is impossible to tell, and she lacks the courage to assert her feelings to the computer, and to ask it how it feels. Yet if the strength of a love which unites exists in proportion to the distance between each lover, then she is typing this sentence—where the buckwheat and coconut flour pancakes she makes are looser and less impressive than the ones she ate in Portland, and where the sunroom projects itself both in and out of her mind like a silent picture—until the computer's keys wrap themselves around her, and until she and its letters are one and the same.

The strawberry-rhubarb compote atop the fucked-up buckwheat and coconut flour pancakes, blended with coconut milk and blueberries and mixed by hand, is made with a tablespoon of the same kind of honey once produced in a poet's New Hampshire backyard. After traveling to Portland, Maine, she drove to New Hampshire with Ian Hatcher as part of a tour of New England wherein they read aloud their literary works for crowded and empty rooms. *1/16 of a tablespoon of honey represents one bee's life*, the poet's partner, the beekeeper, explained to them the morning after their sparsely attended reading at a DIY venue.

In New Hampshire, she slept on a hardwood floor in a cocoon of white blankets. Ian Hatcher slept on a spring-filled mattress above her, level with the honey at rest in oversized glass containers on a folding table at the carriage house's periphery. His sleeping did not make a sound. In the morning, she said his name twice to awaken him— *Ian Hatcher, Ian Hatcher*—once for good luck, once for death. Then they drank coffee in front of a goat and a Christmas tree carcass. "You looked like a caterpillar," he said, referring to her blanket-swaddled body in the night. "You looked the same," she said, lying. Then they entered a car, drove through the woods, and listened to a song that sounded like the most patient form of love.

In a pot over a blue flame, she melts coconut oil with cacao powder and 6 tablespoons of honey like that produced in the poet's New Hampshire backyard. *1/16 a tablespoon of honey represents one bee's life,* the poet's partner explained.

When bees have sex, they do so in midair, like trapeze artists floating without any equipment. Or like ghosts. Or like the porn star who illegally uploaded a video of himself having sex while sky diving. She stirs each tablespoon of honey into the pot, and the mixture becomes warm. Warmth, she imagines while watching two bees copulate outside of her window, is one requisite criterion of bee sex. Of course, there are other, more idiosyncratic features of bee sex, she imagines, though she cannot remember what they are.

She pours the warm mixture into twelve individual cupcake wrappers and Google searches "bee sex" in her computer:

When a lucky drone reaches one of the queens, he mounts her and flexes his abs to extend his endophallus, the bee equivalent of a penis, into the queen's sting chamber, she reads on *National Geographic*'s website. *He releases his semen with such speed and force that there's said to be an audible pop.*

This is the climax of a male's life—and it's rapidly downhill from there.

Then the drone falls down, completely paralyzed, and his bee penis stays behind with the queen. This is what ultimately kills him.

After twenty minutes of reading about bee sex, she puts aside her computer and looks down at the cupcake wrappers, neatly filled with melted cacao powder, coconut oil, and honey. Upon entering the freezer, they will become raw chocolates. As such, they will transcend their classification as simulacra (much like the bee sex JPEGs) thereby becoming hyperreal—of a sleek and flawless body—never existing in reality but, rather, in the dimension within which reality is sustained.

Outside, the real bees will continue having sex, which is neither right nor wrong.

She begins to cook fiddlehead ferns, which she purchased from an essential worker at the food coop while wearing a KN95 mask. She places them into a blue and white bowl that was handmade in Japan before the pandemic started. Prior to blanching them, she boils them in a pot of water. Soon, they are poured over ice. Like a strand of grass, each fiddlehead is bright green, and free from marks or stains. Later, they become abject fiddleheads, fiddleheads covered in soot that ooze soot and that invoke death via their soot, which is composed of amorphous carbon: the chemical element of atomic number six that occurs in impure form and blocks a person's energy. [*Where, then, are we to put the evil?*] Because they are sootstained and oozing poison, she transfers the abject fiddleheads—*abject*, from the Latin *abjection*, invoking a literal throwing away—from the strainer to the trash. As the fiddleheads continue to soot—any noun can be verbed, just as any verb can be objectified, stabilized, made into something that can be inspected, viewed from all sides, and analyzed—her mind turns toward infected fruits, and an image spawns of waste spreading in a wet spring environment, whereby the abject fiddleheads become rendered into the doers of their own actions, just as she will one day become freed from herself, no matter what suffering. Freedom can only be attained by one who is detached—a fiddlehead from its young fern, a drone bee from its endophallus, a person from their body—and there are countless ways to die.

**

There are unpeeled red potatoes she slices into circles and cuts twice: once through the y-axis, once through the x. So too is there a pound of green beans whose fragile tails she breaks. A window is open. The air is poisoned. Time is moving. Her hair is grey and black.

As she slices the freshly broken beans in half, she thinks about the playwright in the desert who once emailed her a ticket to an evening concert by the low voice. Although she only met the playwright once, when she was twenty-three, they have kept in touch on-and-off in the computer for a decade. At times, she studies his picture online—his nose is similar to hers—and reflects upon the peculiarity of human correspondence. It is strange to have a relative stranger be your mirror, and to even feel in some way that you might be related to them (as a long-lost sister or second cousin, for example) even as you may be trying to get them to sleep with you. About the concert ticket, the playwright typed: *Consider it a gift; it's a good coincidence; I love Bill Callahan's music too. You're welcome.*

Framed by plastic trees, the low voice sat on a chair in front of a dark wall covered in icicle lights. *We are constantly on trial / it's a way to be free*, he sang. Simone Weil: *The cross as a balance, a lever.* As she slices each potato twice, she thinks about Jesus kissing Mary Magdalene gently on her lips, expressing his desire to be lifted to a higher plane. She wants to interpret these fragments as signs, to find meaning in this assemblage of seemingly disconnected symbols and events. There exist too many coincidences in patterns, too many synchronicities between people. What is the hidden message?

Red potatoes boil; green beans steam. Outside, the world is crumbling. In conversations, friends repeat this: *the world is crumbling.* Indeed, there are undeniable signs that indicate she is living in an alternative novel universe, such as the fact that the World Heath

Organization has declared a global pandemic, or that countless sirens are resounding every hour, or that each evening her neighbors bang on pots and pans in praise of frontline workers. These facts are coupled with a tacit shame that she is as disturbed by the facts themselves as she is by the death statistics they signify, and that she fills her isolated days with cups of tea, grocery shopping trips, video chats with Ian Hatcher, meandering Google searches, and masturbation. And it is odd to see bees having sex in March while the world is ending.

She downloads instructions to prepare a dressing for the green beans and potatoes: 1/3 cup extra virgin olive oil mixed with 2 tablespoons of sherry vinegar mixed with 1 tablespoon of Dijon mustard mixed with 1 tablespoon fresh lemon juice mixed with 1 clove of minced garlic mixed with salt and pepper to taste. One may add red onion; she opts for an amethyst scallion. Fold or stir. Serve warm or chilled. Plate with finely minced chives. Sprinkle with cumin. Then open the corporately owned social networking application designed to help friends and strangers see what friends and strangers see, and post.

Hon tsai tai flowers are sometimes called *edible rape* on Google. They are yellow and edible and grow in an assemblage reminiscent of a bouquet. Holding a knife, she recites to herself the name of the varietal—*edible rape*—and slices through the plant's stems, trying to imagine them extending underground in a gesture that invokes an exhalation that energetically descends through the spine. It is in tandem with rising energy that this descending energy helps the lungs breathe. In her computer, she performs a cursory search to confirm this: *'rising energy' + 'descending energy' + 'breath' + 'circulation' + 'edible rape.'* An article about whether or not CBD gummies are effective is all she ends up reading.

On descending movement, Simone Weil writes that while gravity makes things come down, wings make them rise. Here, gravity is the force that causes a person to draw back from another the moment the other makes it clear she needs him. Though to need anyone is, from the Old Norse *mistaka*, meaning to take in error, akin to taking in oxygen or how one takes in a solar eclipse through glasses that allow safe viewing of the sun

At once, she recalls assuming the posture of a horse while practicing a specific form of yogic breathing: short, sharp inhalations in and out, out and in; short, sharp breaths in honor of the short, sharp life. This breathing is as much a cleansing exercise as it is an invocation of death. As she cuts the rape flowers—the seed-bearing part of the *hon tsai tai* plant that removes oxygen from the air—she breathes in and out, out and in.

As a teenager, she was frequently cut from productions for which she auditioned—plays, choruses, and pageants—because she was the opposite of pretty. She had matted dark hair, two fangs, premature varicose veins, and a round center. Her varicose veins resembled Orion; like the white of an egg, her gender was runny. How does a hen feel when she's hungry? To Ian Hatcher, she composes a sentence consisting of a memory of a genetically modified chicken breast she pushed toward her mother in protest, and then composes others: a sentence consisting of a memory of trying on a midnight blue evening gown while feeling fat; a sentence about ordering a dozen chicken tenders from a fast food eatery near the interstate; a sentence about eating said chicken tenders in the backseat of a car; a sentence about the ontology of the moniker *chicken tender*—is it a fast food, a form of currency, or a person who tends a chicken?

You may no longer eat chicken tenders :), Ian Hatcher says.

I don't! she replies. Then she composes a sentence containing the sense-memory of one regular-sized bar of chocolate; she composes a sentence containing a bag of freezer-burned berries; she composes a sentence gently coated in flour; she composes a sentence cut in half with the blade of a knife; she composes a sentence that requires no preheating; she composes a sentence labeled *no bake*; she composes a sentence belonging to the pantry; she composes a sentence made of soy; she composes a sentence consisting of a memory of eating fried potatoes with a teenage inamorata. They were both becoming hideous as they gorged.

Her short, sharp life—as punctuated by the short, sharp breath she practices when consciously breathing—is punctuated by short, sharp memories that are ingested as plant matter. As she thinks this, she slices through a cluster of edible rape flowers the color of a yellow sun that, upon making contact with the knife, scatter across the surface of her mind like tumbleweeds. Upon their release, the flowers dissipate into component parts: the style, stamen, ovary, and stigma. The former is a manner of doing; the latter marks a feeling of shame. And the entire assemblage occupies the space between desire and perception, where memory is configured as a series of structural aboveground anatomies that detach themselves from the brain before rapeseeds fall from its rafters and scatter across the stage.

On an eight-mile walk, she considers a series of uncategorizable memories that nevertheless remain archived in her mind. There is, for example, an image of a now-shuttered café where she watched an acquaintance who did not recognize her eat a ham and butter sandwich, and the image of a vegan bakery's interior where she used to hold office hours with students who rarely showed up. There is also the image of a Cuban restaurant where she drank bright pink cocktails with a collaborator who moved away to California one week before the pandemic was officially declared a global emergency, and the image of an Italian restaurant whose solely gluten-free fare she has never actually purchased for herself because a friend who has not texted her back in weeks purchases it for her. Not to mention the image of a wine bar containing one intrusive ancient tuxedo cat (different from the ancient tuxedo cat she met in Portland, Maine), and the image of a dive bar where her coworker once bought her a gin and tonic and touched her knee. Upon realizing her uncategorizable memories are all categorized by food and attachments to other people and one cat, she wonders if memories of her life have always been categorized this way—by food and other people, and the occasional cat—or if her current lifestyle is driving her insane. As she continues walking, her legs grow increasingly tired, and she begins to feel like more of an outline of a person than an actual person—like an object to be clicked and filled in, whose clicking will result in an invisible trail of energy that filters from one memory to the next.

Standing next to a ghost, she slices ornaments for salad: an avocado (green butter), an heirloom tomato (red and black), a black fig (sliced in half), a peach (imported from South Carolina). The blue and white plate in front of her contains a field of leaves in its center. She opens a can of chickpeas (organic, canned, non-BPA lined), spreads them across the field, and adds a handful of blueberries (approximately the color of dark water). The ghost chops parsley. And although she lives in a psychic medium's building, she is not sure whether the ghost is herself, a memory, or the presence of an actual spirit.

Now she is eating her feelings. They look like everything she loves: an avocado, an heirloom tomato, a black fig, a peach. *Who would dream of being against love?*, the cultural critic Laura Kipnis asks. *No one.* On love, Simone Weil writes that the phrase *I love you* can take on varying degrees of significance depending on *the depth of the region in a man's being from which it proceeds without the will being able to do anything.* In this way, love is also a ghost, burgeoning as it does from one's unconscious. She takes a moment to lick fig juice from her fingers, then transcribes the entirety of this quote into a second corporate network, the space in the computer where one's thoughts are shaped by a 280-character constraint.

There are so many generic sentiments she loathes yet desires to hear: *I love you; I'm sorry; I do.* She thinks: what programs do these commands execute in their speakers? What commands do these programs incite in their listeners? Then she thinks about centuries worth of cultural baggage that has been checked on airplanes for the sake of reinforcing the privatization of love with regard to the couple container.

I love you; I'm sorry; I do: imagine a hollow body looking in on itself!

Atop the blue and white plate, the field's shape increasingly resembles an ecosystem: the green leaves are dependent on the avocado as the avocado is dependent on the black fig as the black fig is dependent on the heirloom tomato, and so on until the ecosystem seems to proceed autonomously, in a lyrical feedback loop. In the same way, the generic sentiments she problematizes but desires to recite—*I love you; I'm sorry; I do*—rely on one another's repeated scripts in order to carry on through time and space cyclically. But what happens when *I love you* meets *I love you*, *I'm sorry* meets *I'm sorry*, *I do* meets *I do*? "Thank you for coming in," the food coop's essential worker said in quotation marks at the end of her grocery shopping trip, wherein quotation marks call attention to the artificiality of the essential worker's statement as it is transcribed from the physical world to the page. Upon reciting this phrase, he elaborated no further, nor did she inquire as to what the status of her body as narrated by heirloom tomatoes might imply for her future condition, her severe depression: her programmatic response to life's changing condition, which is both inevitable and that against which she fights by taking a photograph, altering its size, uploading it, and returning to bed.

*
**

To the corporately owned social network designed to help friends and strangers see what friends and strangers see, she uploads a photograph of a blue and white bowl filled with a green liquid smoothie composed of one banana (fair trade), two leaves of kale (organic, bunched with rubber), parsley (the color of a Tyrannosaurus rex), mixed field greens (grown in Vermont), frozen mangoes (cold to the touch), coconut water (slightly pink), and ice (that saps a person's energy). The green liquid smoothie is topped with prepackaged banana nut butter granola ("organic banana puree and superfood seeds coated in cashew butter and coconut oil with hints of vanilla and sea salt"), a sliced peach (the color of a robin's breast), half a banana (fair trade, gently sliced into circles), kiwi (a flightless bird), blueberries (the color of sapphires), strawberries (overripe with firm stems), and almonds (roasted, lightly salted). As ornament, she adds chia seeds, cacao nibs, and shredded coconut to the top of her concoction. After which, she thinks: What do friends and strangers see when they see what she sees? Do the photographs she takes, alters, and uploads online embody her first-person perspective? And if so, is this first-person perspective addressing a second-person *you*? Or does it call out to a third-person—he, she, it, or they—ever-shifting in the midst of a breakdown?

When it comes to perspective, an inherent falsehood is always at play. Simone Weil: *I must necessarily turn to something other than myself since it is a question of being delivered from self.* The third-person is always a first; the second is always talking to myself to you. People employing the first-, second-, or third-person point of view are always without objectivity. Yet if the photographer is lucky, there will be a moment in which differences are put on hold, and a reciprocal desire between the first and the second flourishes. Otherwise, one forages in darkness not only for kale but also for one's own reflection, which is never clearly labeled *one, two,* or *three*, but is instead designated via the sensation of seeing what one can't, loving what can't be, and waiting for the smoothie bowl to blend.

*
**

A riddle:

Sesame seeds are black; chive flowers are purple. Carrots are shredded in the shape of rice noodles. Mizuna is a type of spider mustard green—smooth in texture, feathery in shape. When waiting to say *I love you* to someone, how long is too long to wait?

/

At the riddle's terminal point, she considers a quotation from Simone Weil's notebooks: *Strictly speaking time does not exist, yet we have to submit to it. Whether it is a question of passively borne duration—physical pain, waiting, regret, remorse, fear—or of organized time— . . . we are really bound by unreal chains.*

Sesame seeds. Chive flowers. Carrots. Mizuna. As she eats her Thai crunch salad, she forgets the point of the riddle, and also loses track of Simone Weil's argument. And cries and cries and cries.

To prepare the meal consisting of brown rice capellini punctuated by lacinato kale (the color of a weeping willow's leaves), spring onion (organic, bunched with rubber), garlic (hardneck), purple scallion (like a bite mark or a bruise), hon tsai tai flowers (yellow and wild rape), and heirloom tomatoes (whose shapes resemble jewelry), she brings a pot of water to a boil.

As an algae-covered swimming pool filled with frogs defines the middle of the woods, the pot of boiling water defines the center of the kitchen. Alternatively, the middle of the woods may be defined by a heaping pile of antique mint green gin bottles [*the color of a hospital's walls, a mental institution, a prison*]. Gin, a clear alcoholic spirit distilled from grain and flavored with juniper berries, is the poisonous liquid she drinks prior to entering a dream defined by slurred language and the color black.

Gin tastes like a Christmas tree; glass is fused from sand mixed with lime and soda. The bottle from which she drinks is cold and brittle, a window that keeps its eyes on the world. Through it, she sees herself: a hen carrying her heart, an egg. It is smooth, her egg. It is the color of milk. And its yolk is the color of butter yet presents the appearance of blood. [*The egg which breaks inside the chicken always has the appearance of blood.*] And whereupon she becomes poisoned by drinking too much gin, she enters the abyss, a region of hell conceived as a bottomless pit. And it is into this pit she falls. [*One is condemned to false infinity. That is hell itself.*]

As she falls, she has not a moment to think about stopping.

In lieu of stopping, she continues to fall down what seems to be a very deep pit.

Either the pit is very deep, or she falls very slowly, for she has plenty of time as she goes down to look about her, and to wonder what will happen next. First, she tries to look down and make out what she is coming to, but it is too dark to see. Then she looks at the sides of the pit, and notices that they are lined with cupboards and bookshelves: here and there she sees maps and pictures hung upon pegs: an illustration of Virginia Woolf; an antique map of France; a poster detailing the correct way to make quiche; a letter-pressed poem by one dead poet dedicated to a second dead poet; a black-and-white photograph of a goat. She takes down a jar from one of the shelves as she passes. It is labeled ORANGE MARMALADE but, to her great disappointment, it is empty. She does not drop the jar, for fear of killing somebody underneath, and manages to put it into one of the cupboards as she falls past it.

As she falls, she notices weeds: dandelion, chicory, purslane, white clover, green carpetweed, wood sorrel, common nettle. A blue violet. At first, she does her best to control the weeds by imagining herself pulling them out, and then she thinks of the Zen monk Shunryu Suzuki: *We pull the weeds and bury them near the plant to give it nourishment.* It is painful to notice the weeds, to feel them in hell, which is to say, the mind. They are overgrown and contain her ugliest thoughts—of the fox, the knives, the phrase "the opposite of pretty," and past images of her matted hair, her fangs, her premature varicose veins, and her malnourished center. As she watches the thoughts, she knows they are illusory. There must be a way to pluck them from her mind, to flatten them between the pages of a book until they dry and are ready to be framed in glass.

Down, down, down. Will her fall never come to an end? *I wonder how many miles I've fallen by this time,* she wonders aloud. *I must be getting somewhere near the center. Let me see: the center would be close to earth, I think*—(for, you see, she had learned to recognize the earth by the scent of heirloom tomatoes which, like weeds, she notices and plucks)—*yes, that seems right, but then I wonder what latitude or longitude I've got to?*

In her right palm, she balances one heirloom tomato. In her left, she balances a second. And so it is that she finds herself standing behind a wooden cutting board, her palm clasping the handle of a knife.

As she slices an heirloom tomato through its y-axis—its first-person perspective, the little convex mirror through which the self inverts—the tomato separates into two halves, and one half of it enters into an argument with its other half. The split tomato is akin to two identical twins arguing until one twin begins to scream. [*Though they may have lost their "I," it does not mean they have no more egoism.*]

I should not love my suffering because it is useful, one-half of the tomato says. *I should love it because it is.*

To which the other half responds: *I refuse to make myself suffer.*

At birth, the heirloom tomato emerged as one fruit from one stalk and, as it grew up, its two halves grew apart. Despite their separation, their connection to one another remained, and one day they reunited in a cardboard box. In it, they shared conversation. They discussed their fears; they puzzled over nakedness. They parsed contemporary truths reflected within lies and fantasized about how the essence of being human correlates with one's capacity to take a selfie or a photograph of one's dinner.

We shan't photograph ourselves, one half of the tomato said.

We're not human, stupid, replied the other half.

And besides, the person eating us is the idiot taking our photograph, the one half says. *She is afraid to eat; she is a control freak.*

And all the food coop and health industry rhetoric moralizes her plate, tells her we're "good," the other half says. *But we're not good; we're tomatoes!*

The delusion that she's capturing an accurate representation of us via this photograph convinces her that she's supposedly helping someone see what she sees, the one half says.

When waiting to say *I love you* to someone, how long is too long to wait?

But the fact is, by taking this photograph, she is not seeing. Rather, she is talking to herself to a split heirloom tomato while waiting for them to talk back.

One half of the heirloom tomato tells the other half about the psychiatric ward where vegetables are sent to be treated for clinical depression and borderline personality disorder.

When vegetables dig themselves out of these conditions, one half of the heirloom tomato explains, *they become enveloped by a sense of calm.*

Shut up, the other half of the tomato says, insecure about its lack of calm.

Stop calling attention to your dark spots, says the overly aggressive half of the tomato who is defensive about the importance of mental health services for heirloom tomatoes.

Fuck you.

Fuck you too. You look like a hoe corpse.

It's called blossom end rot.

Dumb slut, shut up. You're talking too much. Hoe corpses like you should be seen and not heard.

You're being a selfish bitch.

I have nothing else to say. You're not worth it.

You fucking cuckoo bitch. You're so crazy.

Worse still, your skin is so thin, as if to transmit light. But all I see is rot.

Cuckoo bitch. You're such a crazy bitch. Shut the fuck up.

You shut the fuck up. Rotten hoe corpse.

The tomatoes argue like this for a very long time before settling down and wondering where the person who cut them open went. Eventually, she picks them up and drops them in blazing hot oil and kills both of them. She is grateful for their silence.

In olive oil, she sautés the garlic and heirloom tomatoes until the heirloom tomatoes shed blood. In a separate pot, she pours water for capellini (a mixture of organic brown rice flour and water) and patiently waits for it to boil. As the water heats, she observes how the heirloom tomatoes—stewed in a cast iron pan opposite to the pan of boiling water—assume a new shape and texture. They are now globular in form, and quiet, and tender.

In a memory, she is eating dinner with a group of strangers in the middle of the woods. These strangers happen to be her colleagues at an artist residency, and they also happen to be drunk on liquids of various colors: amber, gold, salmon. She is twenty-four years old and drinking carbonated water. This is one of the only memories from the woods that she will recall. Nearby, in an algae-covered swimming pool, frogs are singing, a form of protection. Unlike frogs, she is always quiet in groups.

As her dining companions' drunkenness increases, their laughter intensifies, and so too does their discourse. They are talking about critical theory in specialized terms, including *objet petit a*, *lack*, *scansion*, and *signification*. They interrupt and layer their voices atop one another until their choir assumes the prosody of frogs. Politely (she likes to imagine), she evades contributing to their song. In truth, she is a snob. It has always exhausted her to react and respond while people speak. Not to mention how heavy the feeling weighs that she needs to contribute her voice to this sort of academic group dynamic. How is she to tell stories when frogs are using a specialized vocabulary? The stories she fails to share today do not define her, she reminds herself. For the story she does not tell will be different tomorrow, anyway. For example, if she tells the following story—

One summer, I picked an heirloom tomato from someone else's community garden plot. The next day, I found a plastic mannequin hand resting where the heirloom tomato had been. I immediately purchased another heirloom tomato at the farmer's market and placed it in the mannequin's hand as a peace offering. For weeks, the replacement heirloom tomato remained in the mannequin's hand, where it slowly decomposed and rotted.

—one might imagine she is telling it with a lesson in mind. But what if she is telling this story solely for its precise imagery, or for the feeling of emptiness the story invokes, or for the way the social contract between community gardeners breaks in the story, or so the moment of time the story captures does not become lost? She is also obsessed with the plastic hand in the story and the fact it will outlive her and all her creations, culinary and otherwise, because that is what plastic does. Disgusting, she thinks.

Should she tell this story, the frogs would stop singing and stare back at her blankly.

As she plates the capellini (a mixture of organic brown rice flour and water), she focuses on juxtapositions and color: fifty percent of a bright pink fig at the top of the bowl; fifty percent of a blood red heirloom tomato at the bottom. To the left is a bouquet of edible rape flowers (yellow and wild); to the right, a cluster of micro-greens (whose assemblage creates a miniature bouquet). The center is the space for chili flakes (crushed red), chives (the color of a fern's leaves), salt (grey), and pepper (black).

Upon noticing her heirloom tomato's blossom end rot, she is reminded of the last time she entered a bathroom and mutilated her own flesh. There was no specific urge driving this act beyond the echo of a voice in her mind. *Your skin is so thin, as if to transmit light,* she heard it say. Then the voice called her a cuckoo bitch and a dumb slut. Then it told her to shut the fuck up.

What ghosts live inside her?

In this paragraph, she invokes the ghost of her mother, and her mother's mother, and her mother's mother's mother. Her mother's mother was hungry once, during the second World War. And her mother was hungry too. So her mother cooked a chicken breast and ate it. As it cooked, she watched it, and thought of the years that pass in a life. So many years, so little life. And the chicken dried out as she thought this, which wasn't because the oven was too hot, but because time was passing. Then a third ghost was summoned: the ghost of a ghost—a great-aunt—who slaughtered herself in a bathroom, as she (whose book is a life) is thinking about cutting herself. The ghost of a ghost—her great-aunt—cut herself to death because her husband cheated on her, which she—Claire (whose book is a life)—dislikes on the principle of her feminist values. But she also empathizes with the act, and sees it as deeply tragic. Claire also realizes she is haunted by the ghost of her dead great-aunt, and that this ghost sometimes makes her want to kill herself, which makes her feel ashamed.

Once again, she considers slicing the knife against her fore-arm—once for good luck, once for death, and once for her cheated upon great-aunt—and imagines her own tattoo, an empty set, { }—raising from the dead like embossed typography. While she envisions a pool of blood surrounding her, she throws away the heirloom tomato, renounces its blossom end rot, and puts the ghost to rest, subsequently having a dream about the poet Lothario who would cook her meals before driving her cuckoo and cheating on her with a professional clown.

After plating the meal consisting of brown rice capellini (tender card-board), lacinato kale (the color of a weeping willow's leaves), spring onion (organic, bunched with rubber), garlic (hardneck), purple scallion (like a bite mark or a bruise), heirloom tomatoes (whose shapes resemble jewelry), and edible rape flowers (yellow and wild), she takes a photograph. She adjusts its brightness and vantage point, then uploads it to a website where it becomes a point of data via which her life may be objectified, stabilized, made into something that can be inspected, viewed from all sides, and analyzed.

Though the photograph is symmetrical and pleasing in its color palette, it does not reveal the flavor of the pasta, made rancid by the flavor of the wine much in the same way a couple's fucking is made rancid by the flavor of alcohol. Fucking is a dialogue between two or more entities trying to imagine themselves into one another. As such, the brown rice capellini attempts to locate itself in the lacinato kale, and the lacinato kale imagines itself reflected in a single amethyst scallion. At the center of this imagining is the human, a vampire in search of a meal. *We love someone*, Simone Weil writes, *that is to say, we love to drink his blood*. So one anticipates the warmth of another as a point of comfort, only to be torn to shreds. Oh, we are hungry. And the meat is so cold.

/

Dream-content: Once upon a COVID-19 winter, she was infatuated with a poet Lothario. He was fleetingly infatuated with her too, but all it really did was fuck her. In the dream, she is sleeping over at his shack for the final time when she finds a scrunchie underneath the pillow on his bed beneath which she stored her nightshirt. The scrunchie is beige and satin and circular: a sort of flaccid fabric penis wrapping around itself as a metaphor whose poetics invoked a VIP wristband.

"She's a professional clown," the poet Lothario says when she asks him what this object is, albeit the object to which he is referring is the woman and not the scrunchie, which lacks a pronoun and thus is gender-neutral despite its feminine connotations. He relays that the professional clown is another woman who recently slept in his bed, though he insists that it was not amorous.

Looking him in the face, she stretches out the scrunchie to full capacity and pulls it over her head until it clings to her neck like a noose. This is the first image in the dream that is not her actual lived experience during the COVID-19 pandemic, during which she was actually infatuated with a man she believed possessed power in the literary world; with whom she shared snacks every few days; who had an erudite book collection and taught her some things about international literature; whose bed she made each time she slept over; who blew smoke on her; and with whom she believed at the time she was in love. While the relationship felt like a totalizing experience within the COVID-19 pandemic, it also felt like being in a play. And as in a play, each performed moment felt rehearsed, but not by her, as she did not possess the play's script. Indeed, she was completely alone throughout these experiences with the poet Lothario, who despite his sloppiness seemed to somehow also carefully calculate each of his scenes. A fast-burning candle placed here; a beige scrunchie or flaccid fabric penis wrapping around itself there. A bathroom cupboard containing used toothbrush after used toothbrush, as if curated by Bluebeard. Yet after a few years of processing their months together, time edited away his presence from her memory of the pandemic, as well as his power. This left her alone in her apartment with a carrot salad.

She does not bother to pull out her hair from beneath the

scrunchie. It is tight and suffocating, a disgusting shade of beige, and not even made of actual silk. As she strangles herself, the sloppy pervert looks at her with a gentle smile on his face. She begins to turn purple but nevertheless keeps the scrunchie around her neck until she begins to hallucinate that it is a flaccid penis strangling her. And since this is a dream, the scrunchie becomes a flaccid penis strangling her. At which point she wakes up, gasping for breath.

She prepares two blueberry muffins sans eggs, wheat, and dairy. First, she conjures a flax egg: ½ tablespoon flaxmeal (golden) combined with 2 tablespoons of water (translucent), which she sets aside to congeal as she combines her dry ingredients— ¾ cup gluten-free flour (the color of gluten-free flour); 2 ½ tablespoons brown sugar (brown); ½ teaspoon baking soda (bright white, like cocaine); a pinch of salt (cocaine)—and her wet ingredients: 4 tablespoons almond milk (sort of white); ½ teaspoon vanilla (rum-colored, strong smelling); 1 tablespoon melted vegan butter (gentle). Ultimately, she merges these ingredients, and subsequently adds ¼ cup of blueberries (the color of globe thistle, grape hyacinth, or forget-me-nots), and divides the batter into two ramekins whose walls are lightly buttered. These ramekins rest atop the oven's middle shelf and are illuminated by a small light via which she watches the muffins rise.

Those look so good :)), Ian Hatcher texts after she sends him a photograph of the muffins. In the Pacific Northwest, he is drinking a cup of stinging nettle tea. He texts her a photograph of it, which she wishes she could drink with her muffins.

It's not who or what we eat, but how. She is thinking through this axiom: love and hunger. Desire and thirst. Cannibalism in relation to sexual appetite. Simone Weil posited that to love another is a phenomenon of the former, that *the force in love is the rage of our own hunger to use the other as a means to fill (or at least conceal) our psychological voids.*

[*Beloved beings…provide us with comfort, energy, a stimulant. They have the same effect on us as a good meal after an exhausting day of work. We love them, then, as food.*] She is frying tofu (crafted by hand) with mango sauce (not from a can). First, she boils water and wild rice (long grain brown, sweet brown, wild, and whole grain black). Second, she lowers the flame. Next, she drains the cube of tofu, wraps it in towels made of paper through which the tofu's water seeps. Now it is ready to be sliced into cubes: y-axis, y-axis, y-axis, y-axis; x-axis, x-axis, x-axis, x-axis. Where is the "z"? She considers the knife, of which she is as fearful as she is reverent. When she is done carving, she immediately runs the instrument under water, hangs it over the stove on the magnetic strip where other knives reside.

In late June, she visited a restaurant with Ian Hatcher, who had not yet moved to the Pacific Northwest. Together, they sat inside a poorly ventilated outdoor vestibule constructed from what seemed to be cardboard, wire, and super glue. They ordered cold noodles. Their bodies were hot. Their hands did not touch. As they looked over their menus, they discussed rendering creatures in three-dimensional landscapes, and the formlessness that accompanies grief. Ian Hatcher told her about his parents' chicken coop. She told him about the poet Lothario with whom she was infatuated. The noodles they ordered were covered in sesame oil. Her body was turned at an angle. His existed on the z-axis. Together, they speculated as to whether anyone in the vicinity was on a date. Were they? It was a good day; it was impossible to know.

To prepare the mango sauce, she places one cup of sliced mango (the color of a citrus fruit) in a cup with lime juice (tart), cumin (gold), and tamari (gluten-free). To this cup, she attaches a powerful blade. It is late in the evening, and the blender makes sounds like screaming. Outside, America sounds like the war zone it is. Strangers are shooting fireworks, which emit a vibration that defines her country's so-called independence, its irrevocable second amendment. As she clears a path between the sink and the stove, she thinks about mass murder, and how this celebration of people gathered could be interrupted at any time by spraying bullets. She imagines a crowd of people around her: babies in strollers with bare feet; couples holding hands, a symbol of their being chainlinked; still lifes of tourists atop rental bikes holding sticks and staring at themselves through pocket-sized rectangles, as if their faces were plates covered in vegetables and not KN95 masks.

She walks to and from the counter, then begins chopping. After she chops, she joins a protest several hundred feet from the site of that evening's forthcoming fireworks display. This protest, organized in response to the countless murders of Black people by police across the nation, takes place in front of a restaurant where diners are eating beneath a bright yellow canopy. The protestors face the diners, who face off. One diner crosses her legs, lowers her gaze. Another pushes dead meat across the surface of her plate. As the protest takes place, a leader recites names. The protest is punctuated by an indictment of the New York Police Department, who have yet to be indicted by anyone.

Now the New York Police Department is standing behind her—[*she slices an onion*]—and she can feel their weaponry—[*she slices another*]—how they are wanting to shoot. As the protest takes place, the entire neighborhood is grey, covered in light mist and firework explosions.

*
**

On July 4th, she boils water for rice (sorted and cleansed of its dust). It is just before sunset, and her body is tired. As the water boils, she lays in bed and stares at the ceiling. The light source affixed to it resembles the shape of a breast.

Everything needs food to live, even love, the Zen monk says. *If we don't know how to nourish our love, it withers.* RIP Thich Nhat Hanh, not yet dead…

But my tiredness removed me from the substance of the world!

Tiredness has a broad heart, purports Maurice Blanchot.

Or, the philosopher Byung-Chul Han writes that tiredness lends to things an aura of friendliness. When one is tired, *things flicker, twinkle, and vibrate at the edges.* If I am tired in your company, I am not tired *of* you, I am tired *with* you.

Still gazing at the ceiling, she listens to the water boil. *When is water boiling? When, indeed, is water water,* she thinks to herself, repeating fragments of M.F.K. Fisher, then closes her eyes. Her bedroom is quiet; the boiling water is not. Alongside it, she desires to sleep as dust, to erect a door inside her mind that opens toward a body of water whose waves ebb and flow in a state of temporary calm: a cloud of tiredness, an ethereal tiredness, a peaceful lacuna that holds her together and binds her with another in waking life and in sleep, then.

In a dream, she chops ornaments: a spring onion (white like the ceiling), garlic (minced), chives (the shade of wheatgrass or a palm). Using the sharpest knife, she slices twelve leaves of lacinato kale (organic, bunched with rubber), taking special care to carve away the spine. Then she handpicks two bouquets of miniature yellow flowers—*hon tsai-tai,* or edible rape—that she uses to accent the year.

As water boils, does rice dream?

In a dream, she is swimming, but there is no water.

In a dream, she is asleep, and her sleep is a boundary, a wall.

Asleep, she is at a fish store surrounded by aquariums.

Is she a fish, or is she a human?

She looks down: there are fish on the floor.

As such, she surmises, I must be human?

In her mind, she tries to step around the fish [*swimming without swimming*] until there are so many on the floor [*she wakes up*] the dream becomes a nightmare.

To the fish, she transmits a love letter: I am not tired *of* you, I am tired *with* you.

Now tiredness is her friend.

Now she is writing her friend, Ian Hatcher, a letter.

This letter's alphabet moves across the page yet becomes static. Slowly it traverses from one location to the next. There's a magic to the progression. The letter is time outside of time.

When this letter is sent, her love will be drained.

But the alphabet will twinkle on the page:

ABCDEFGHIJKLMNOPQRSTUVWXYZ!

And the location of her feelings will be postmarked.

They will again be in the world.

While Ian Hatcher typically finds photographs of food offensive, he really likes hers. He types this statement from an altitude of 36,000 to 40,000 feet—he is flying back to the Pacific Northwest—and imbues an emoticon—:)—to indicate a standard smile. Like most animals, he is hungry. The contents of her mint green bowl look like edible art, he says. To which she responds with a quote via M.F.K. Fisher: *There are many ways to love a vegetable. The most sensible way to love it is well-treated.*

Ian Hatcher is very impressed. He is glad she is composing vegetables. From afar, she is doing so many wonderful things.

Hovering above it—and what is *it*? The boiled water with black rice to which she adds miso and fried scallions? The center of the oil in which an onion caramelizes? A handful of toasted black sesame seeds she holds in the palm of her hand like a dead bird's corpse?— she selects the sharpest knife and carves a corncob. As she carves, she imagines the knife's potential to sever not only corn, but also flesh and limbs—and vital organs. To whom or what is she bound? Later, she will take one capsule of 5-HTP (200 mg, gluten-free, vegan), a pill that replenishes serotonin levels and causes a person to dream about destination resorts covered in snow. *Those capsules make one's dreams so vivid*, Ian Hatcher says, *I cannot stand to take them.*

As the corn bathes in cast iron clad in hot oil, she plucks leaves from a bouquet of thyme and thinks about her period. It is the color of paprika, or a plateau of conceptual boulders representing her desire, atop which fresh berries are smeared. *Violence is permissible, even occasionally desirable*, she thinks. Her period is painful and incites in her a quiet sense of freedom, but this sense of freedom is not akin to the sense of freedom she once felt at Quaker meetings, where she sat in a room full of pews facing one another, closed her eyes, and focused on channeling her so-called "inner light." There was no food before or after Quaker meeting, as she attended meetings on a weeknight when worship was informal. As such, this worship did not feel like worship at all. Rather, it felt like sitting in silence and recounting faces in her mind of everyone she's ever loved. So too did it feel like gazing at a single sunflower, which existed in a vase in the center of a wooden table adjacent to a pew. This sunflower appeared to be singing or screaming. It was not weeping, for the sunflower did not yet know the gravity of the world.

*
**

Three recipes transcribed from a notebook she does not remember keeping:

LYCHEE

1 lychee

Remove lychee from plastic bag using only two fingers. Grasp firmly, taking care to not let it drop to the floor. Run the skin of your finger along its wallpaper, the skin of a dinosaur. This texture indicates lychee may be warm-blooded. With your sharpest fingernail, pierce the skin and peel it until only translucent flesh remains. Then place the lychee in your mouth and tear its meat with your teeth until you are left with only the seed. To plant a tree, swallow it. To remain barren, do the opposite.

SUNFLOWER BUTTER

1 sunflower
1 stick of non-dairy butter

Extract the sunflower from its vase, and the stick of butter from its gold wrapper. Unfold the gold wrapper out across the kitchen counter as if it were a blanket. The gold portion of the wrapper should face down. Subsequently, tear the petals from the sunflower, and spread them across the kitchen counter and around the gold wrapper, atop which you should perpendicularly place the sunflower stem (which remains attached to the sunflower's center), so these objects intersect one another at an angle of ninety degrees on their given plane. At the end of this sculpture, the sunflower's petals will surround the wrapper, and you will carry a cold stick of non-dairy butter in the palm of your hand.

HONEY DIPTYCH

1 bumblebee
2 fingers

The center of the bee's mouth is rendered visible via the lens that allows one to focus in and in and in. In contrast, the tip of a human index finger is slight—the size of a bee—and when a person runs it along the axis of another human index finger's tip, there is electricity. Between the bumblebee and the human index finger's tip, honey exists. It is a sweet liquid made from flower nectar. And so one can imagine honey running between one finger and the second, because there are only two fingers in this scene, as there are two beings, in contrast to one bumblebee who gently sits atop an echinacea flower in a park, sucking the same flower as a butterfly.

There is no sunflower butter in this story. There is only red cabbage (chopped in strips, the color of late '90s lipstick), caramelized onion (organic, thinly sliced), and imported mango the color of North Point Press's printing of M.F.K. Fisher's collection of culinary essays, *The Gastronomical Me.* She slices it—the red cabbage? the imported mango? the book?—into pleasant shapes she arranges at the bowl's periphery, then places black sesame seeds over it—less for taste than for color, less for color than decor—and takes a photograph, which is forty-nine percent for her and fifty-one percent for you. [*Self-satisfaction over a good action (or a work of art) is a degradation of higher energy. That is why the left hand should not know . . .*] Then she softly smiles and eats dinner with the knowledge she will be better for it, in her spirit and her body too, and will never have to worry about her own love becoming a vegetable.

/

She is thinking about letting vegetables burn as one might let unrequited love smolder, for she is in love with that which burns without a flame.

To prepare three eggs with molten yolks, she boils water for five minutes, then ladles each egg into the pan so their shells graze only the bottom of the pan. In other words, she takes care not to shatter the eggs, so that each egg may live underwater with its siblings as a whale lives underwater with its pod, cultivating a unique language that can only be understood between them, bobbing up and down, half-asleep, while making cooing sounds that stretch across the ocean. How odd, she thinks, that a whale is an egg and vice-versa—not because this conflation is in and of itself a strange thing, but because it—the fact that a whale is equal to an egg and vice-versa—has not occurred to her before the preparation of this meal. *Why didn't I see it before,* she thinks, studying the eggs: first one, then two, then the third, and the fourth, followed by the entire assemblage. [*Probably one of the most private things in the world is an egg until it is broken.*]

The last time she tried preparing eggs with molten yolks, her timing was imperfect. [*One must continually watch what one is doing, without being carried away by it.*] The eggs were undercooked—their yolks were more than runny, a fact she discovered upon suturing the egg's yolk, watching as it broke open and spilled. As the yolk separated and poured away from its white, she thought: *Now the egg is vanquished.*

As the eggs boil for eight minutes, she prepares an ice bath for them in a pale blue bowl. She will even find a moment to cut a scallion (the color of an amethyst) on the bias, thereby bringing into the world elegant, oval-shaped ornaments to rest atop the meal sited in the mint green bowl *[the color of a hospital's walls, a cuckoo house... cnsjglghrul;;s].* Subsequently, she will eat the meal at a stainless-steel table overlooking the church across from her apartment. A rhizome splayed across a nearby wall will move with the breeze.

After dinner, a ghost with whom she has fallen out-of-touch will write to her on the corporate social networking application that feels like a pile of trash in the sea. *Claire,* the ghost will say, but because Claire will be cooking, she will not reply. Hours after writing, the ghost will die while driving a car. Nothing further than this will be specified to Claire. For years, she will not forgive herself for not responding, though she knows the ghost would have empathized. (Says the dictionary: *If you tell an empathetic person that your heart is broken, she might touch her own heart*—that the ghost was an organ donor, then, forms a circle around the narrative.) Her own heart is heavy for the ghost's friends and family, and for everyone who ever loved the ghost, and as she feels her heart grow heavier, she thinks about the ways everyone is out of sync with one another, alone together in spaces virtual and physical, psychic and prophetic. Death is a mirror of time, and life is not as heavy as it seems. While we're here, let's try to be light to one another, she thinks. Then Claire, as the egg, hatches.

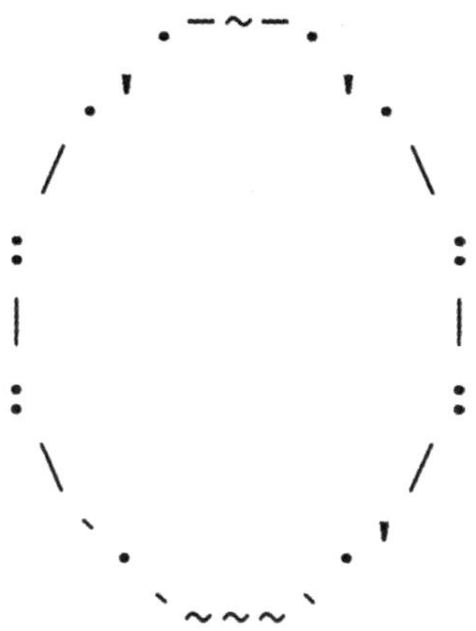

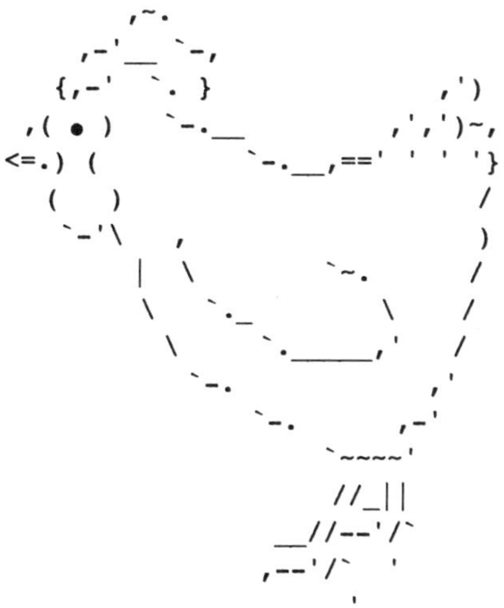

*
**

Claire is waiting for a batter consisting of chickpea flour (the consistency of very fine sand), water (not boiling), olive oil (still a virgin), cumin (gold dust) and salt (Himalayan, pink, and crystal) to set at room temperature while she—like it, the setting batter—sprawls out across her bed. A glass of water sits on her nightstand, and Claire's hands form a semi-circle just beneath her navel. She is tired; her chest rises and falls with the rhythm of her breath. Her eyes are closed. Her feet are bare. Her toes, erect. In this scene, Claire's tiredness exists in relationship to the moon. There is always a resemblance between the earth and the sky, the land and the air, and air the water. The water turns into air; the air turns batter into bread.

*
**

Another recipe that corresponds to the previous page:

SOCCA

> *1 cup chickpea flour*
> *1 cup + 2 tbsp water*
> *¾ tsp salt*
> *1 + ½ tbsp olive oil (for batter)*
> *1 tbsp olive oil (for cast iron pan)*
> *⅛ tsp cumin*

Combine dry ingredients in a bowl. Enter wet into the ocean. In the ocean—your sole interlocutor—you stand. You seethe. You punch its waves. Its temperature is hot, and the conversation taking place between you is a fistfight without hands. Beat until batter is even, then let the batter sit. After at least two hours, return to it. In a broiler, heat a cast iron pan. Pour in olive oil, followed by the batter, which will broil in the broiler until its crust is blackened like a fish. Adjacent to the sea, this gluten-free flatbread is often served with wine. Full of sound and fury, carry your socca and reflect on private sorrow.

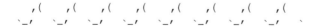

*
**

Claire falls asleep asking sleep to reveal an answer, but all she dreams about is a shack the color of a paper bag. There is no kitchen in it, and she is desperately trying to frame it in her mind as a possible point of transition: a space to rest her body in the middle of her life's third decade, which is neither crystalline nor made of shrubbery, but of a warm light that spreads across the surface of her bed, indicating a spirit presence.

👻 boo

*
**

The novel is a camera, and these words—their settings, props, lighting, costumes, makeup—are its *mise-en-scène.*

As she brings the first bite of forbidden rice and egg to her lips, Claire presses play thirty minutes and fifty-nine seconds into Věra Chytilová's *Daisies,* a 1966 film about two girls, both named Marie, who decide to be rotten. After all, the whole world is rotten! And this world is rotten too. Amidst trash, *Daisies* is uploaded to a website that allows users to watch videos posted by other users, and to upload videos of their own. These videos may be purged by moderators—trash becoming trash—or they may, like *Daisies,* exist with poor vertical resolution: 240 lines drawn in each frame, resulting in a pixelated image.

Thirty minutes and fifty-nine seconds into this video, two young women—both named Marie—set paper decorations on fire. Marie I is wearing a floral dress. Marie II is wearing a halo of flowers around her blonde head. *We're on fire,* they exclaim, bobbing up and down.

Paper decorations burn; a black rotary telephone rings. *Julie, is that you?* a voice says. *Yes, it's me,* both Maries coo. In the background, a chorus sings. Both Maries laugh and rest the phone off its hook. *Julie, I keep thinking about you*—the voice again; and now the Maries ambivalently lounge on a bed. There is the image of an orange on the bed; the room continues to burn around the bed; burnt paper floats in the room, landing on the bed—*I must have fallen in love with you. You don't know what that sleepless night with you means to me. Julie, I keep waiting for you.*

Marie I uses a makeshift skewer—a fork attached to a long stick—to remove a pickle from a jar of dark green vinegar. The voice: *I'm afraid I might never see you again.* Marie II lies down on the bed; a halo of flowers encircles her head. She is propped up on her forearms and holds a pair of scissors to which a hollow metal circle is affixed. Her eyes are bruised with makeup.

Don't treat me like this when you know I love you.

Marie I holds the pickle up to Marie II who, using a pair of scissors, slices it in half.

Are you there? Are you upset with me? Close-up of the black rotary telephone, and the image of Marie II slicing sausage—one, two, three times down its x-axis—before chewing it with her open mouth. *Forgive me, but life without you is torture.*

The Maries each pierce a morsel of sausage using their respective skewers (the ad hoc fork for Marie I; a pair of scissors for II), and consume the meat. *You don't belong to this century*, the subtitle says, and the camera cuts to a shot of the floor, ablaze with paper decorations, accented by a single green apple.

Now Marie II is slicing a hard-boiled egg—one, two, three, four, five times down its y-axis. *I love you Julie. I wouldn't have believed it possible*, the subtitle says. Marie I's foot exists against Marie's II thigh, which exists under the specter of the egg. With her skewer, Marie I lifts a piece of the egg to her mouth, removes it tenderly with her hand, and chews. *Now I know what love is.*

Marie I looks up, blinks five times. *Another piece of meat*, she says. At which point Marie II attempts to slice off her toe with scissors.

What are you doing? I says.

There's no meat around here, II says.

Cut to an image of a fork poking her stomach just above the elastic waist of her white underwear.

What about this?

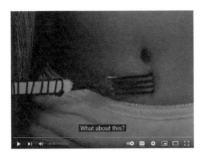

No, I only want fruit now.

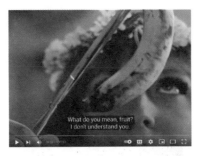

II picks up a rotting banana using her scissors. *What do you mean, fruit?* the subtitle says. She looks up at the banana, then cuts through its center. *I don't understand you.* She cuts it again—*say you'll come again*—and again. As she cuts, the banana's innards squeeze out like paste in a tube; following these incisions, she nibbles on its stem. *Do you hear, Julie?*

Marie I sits up, crosses her legs: *I still fancy something.*

Marie I and II begin looking at a torn-out magazine page. Its glossy surface reflects light; atop it is an image of a cooked chicken lying down on a plate against a bright red background.

Domestic fowl, I says.

I've fallen in love with you, the voice says.

A nice chicken, she says.
My little chicken!

Marie II continues to sort through torn-out magazine pages. On the next is an image of a second meal: a steak in the center of a plate, an advertisement for a restaurant named Thommy's.

That's too big, I says.

A nice steak, II says.

Yes, a nice little steak, I says.

On a nice little piece of bread, II says, and begins to cut the image of a raw steak out from a third advertisement.

Yes, I've got some nice bread at home, the male voice says. *Julie, I love you.*

Bored, Marie I pierces the paper steak with her skewer.

Say you won't treat me like you did last time.

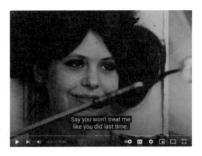

With two hands, she raises the paper steak to her mouth where, for a millisecond, it resembles a pair of lips. She smiles, bites down, chews.

I wouldn't have believed it possible. It's never happened to me before.

She chews and chews and chews—one, two, three, four, five, six, seven, eight, nine, ten, eleven times—blinks, and swallows. Then her eyes widen in abject confusion. Like the phone off its hook, she lies down on the bed.

I think I now know what lo...

Mirroring Marie I, Marie II also lies down, exposing her white bra and underwear to the camera, the ceiling. As she does, her back presses against the phone. Click.

The line goes dead.

*
**

Rewatching *Daisies* on mute, Claire streams a song, "I Bite Through It" by Oneohtrix Point Never, in an attempt to illuminate something new in each of the frame's 240 lines. The song sounds like bullets of mixed realities: a first-person shooter, a spectacle of explosives that opens up into the sky—in fact, the ocean—in fact, an artificial tropical reef located at the Aquarium of the Pacific in Long Beach, California—in fact, a live-streaming simulacrum located at:

*http://www.aquariumofpacific.org/exhibits/tropical_pacific_gallery/
webcam_tropical_reef*

Here, dozens of fish [*the color of an egg's yolk*] swim through the song and through the video on mute and toward her food, where light descends from the sky into the mint green bowl [*the color of aaaaaaaaaaaaaaaaaa*], and where there is a visible sacrifice—the ████████████████████ken bears in life—and where everything in the ocean glimmers.

I I I I I I I I

I
I
I
I
I
I
I

I (bite through it)
I (bite through)
I (bite through it)
I (bite through)
I (bite through it)

After consuming the contents of a glass jar filled to the brim with ¼ cup chia seeds (like microscopic bugs), ¼ cup coconut water (tinted pink), ¾ cup coconut milk (the color of snow), 1 teaspoon vanilla extract (a light perfume), and a touch of agave nectar (concentrated juice from a succulent plant), Claire (who has found her name) stands in the Atlantic Ocean and thinks about how to bring a pot of water to a boil, and how to love while consenting to distance—how to, as Simone Weil writes, *adore the distance between herself and that which she loves*, social and otherwise.

In the ocean—her sole interlocutor—Claire stands. She seethes. She punches its waves. Its temperature is hot, and the conversation taking place between them is a fistfight with only one set of hands. M.F.K. Fisher: *When is water boiling? When, indeed, is water water?* Full of sound and fury, she carries her crosses—her eggs—and reflects on private sorrow. Her greatest character flaw, she thinks, is being quiet, followed by the belief that one can speak without words. [*Though one does not speak, one does not hear either; though one may be telling the truth, there is no further need for pretense.*] Followed closely, then, by evasion, followed by the propensity to fall in love with imaginary objects, a fact against which she was explicitly cautioned by the astrological website where one plugs one's birthdate, place, and time into a form in order to track one's compatibility with a person. Based on its calculations, the website returns its predictions—*your relationship may be very good or very unreal; you must ascertain whether the spiritual quality you perceive is an illusion*; or *you will have spectacular disagreements.* All the while, she stands in the ocean and feels her fury boil, as if it is progressing from fury to fury with something in it. This is her worst quality: to imagine fury contains an object when it is, in fact, a sensation that attaches itself to something.

Today, Claire's life is a lake, still and clear, punctuated by silence. She stands alone, practicing solitude. In precarity, she maintains a spreadsheet detailing her daily expenses, and rations food. *To feel empty is a product of my ancestry,* she thinks to herself, recalling how her French grandparents went hungry following the war.

Thirst and hunger. Blood and bone.

An ambience that reconfigures how we think of character and plot.

This documentary is about a documentarian who lost a family member, and for whom this impression of grief forms a lens via which she comes to consider Simone Weil. Weil is a philosopher with whom the documentarian is so obsessed; therefore, she hires an actress to play her so she can speak to Weil in person herself. These scenes are unsettling. Are they also captivating? Claire cannot make up her mind, though she appreciated the movie due to its autobiographical

"I" juxtaposed with Simone Weil's life story.

As she adds the spices and water and greens to the pot, she thinks about *pain*, the French word for bread. It has been a long day.

How does one relay the events of a year? Claire cracked open, then smeared her yolk against the world. For months, it felt like she couldn't physically do anything, although she sometimes read books, sometimes watched movies. When she was obligated to work, she worked. And she was competent at work—well-regarded for it, in fact. So much so that, along the way, she was awarded for her efforts. Did no one realize how she had cracked? About the hand that broke her, someone said, *That isn't love*, and she thought, *If not, then what?* Now she knows better. Now, cooling off, she eats dinner alone, takes a walk. She goes to acupuncture; she practices psychoanalysis; she attends Quaker meetings; she sits Zazen; she records music; she takes photographs. She lies down on the grass in the park and decomposes.

And then one day, she meets another egg and gets a double yolk.

And the next, she meets a second egg and gets a second double yolk.

An egg walks into a bookstore. Its finances are slim. So she considers stealing a book about salad. But upon considering the ceiling, covered as it is in surveillance apparatuses, she decides against kleptomania (the bookstore is local, after all) and leaves the store behind. As she exits, she considers the bookstore's window display: cookbook, cookbook, cookbook, memoir. *I am outside this though, having the feeling of depression,* she thinks to herself. Then she remembers the excitement she felt upon stealing a black-and-white striped shirt from a nearby box store and regrets not stealing the book. Then she regrets stealing an umbrella from a commons and spending much of the year granting nothing to herself while simultaneously getting so wrapped up in herself, she could only see an ugly mirror, an unkind ghost. Then she goes back into the bookstore, steals the book, and eats it.

Cooking is a form of writing, and vice-versa—if you don't feel like writing the food you cook, your cooking and writing practices are not in alignment. Like cucumbers in vinegar, one must let writing ferment.

She spreads open her book, extracts its yolk, and eats that too, and they conjoin 11:11!!!! Here is a red rose I got for you 🌹 :)

    I got you one too 🌹 :)

    You are my twin flame

    What's that?

    I got you this link too :)

    Thanks Claire :)

    https://www.twinflames1111.com/blog/faq/doc1#

The year is still 2020. It will not always be 2020.

At this time, it remains unclear why she has begun to eat chicken.

As a teenager, she read a Buddhist primer about reincarnation, and stopped eating meat.

Soon, she became an ethical vegan.

She taught classes about her dietary restrictions and referred to her subject as *critical animal studies*.

At restaurants, she proudly boasted of her lack: *I do not eat meat, fish, dairy, eggs, gluten.*

Months earlier and

several aisles away, her ex-partner broke the news of their own
    veganism.
She remembers standing in front of the ice cream case, staring into
    its ice cream.
At the time, she did not understand why, but in retrospect she
    understands:

    • avoidance
    • ~~constraining one's diet due to despair~~
    • dietary restrictions
    • ~~food angst~~

Into a box titled "Find & Replace," she types: *chicken*. The search brings back thirteen results:

1. The book's title.

2. An epigraph by Clarice Lispector, translated by Giovanni Pontiero.

3. *The egg is the chicken's great sacrifice. The egg is the cross the chicken bears in life.*

4. The phrase "a brood of backyard chickens."

5. *A chicken has been killed by a fox.*

6. A violent scene featuring a fox "tearing open a rabbit wire fence surrounding a brood of chickens with its teeth, gaining entrance, then grabbing a hen in its mouth and tearing it apart like tissue paper." At the end of this scene, she writes, "There's something erotic about it."

7. An anecdote about meeting a brood of backyard chickens in Portland, Maine.

8. A quotation: *The egg which breaks inside the chicken has the appearance of blood.*

9. The image of a row of chickens hanging upside-down from the ceiling of a slaughterhouse.

10. A scene featuring her cooking a chicken breast.

11. The image of chicken drying out.

12. A rhetorical question: *Which came first, the chicken or the greens?*

13. An image of six pieces of chicken.

She was never the egg; she was always the chicken. Everything about oneself—all of the choices one makes—are already pre-written. (I don't know if I actually believe that.) And therefore she must consume herself entirely. (Why? Maybe she didn't have to do that...)

On PsychCentral.com, she takes an eighteen-question online auto-mated quiz to help determine if she should see a mental health pro-fessional for the diagnosis and treatment of depression.

Then again, she thinks, I may be projecting an extreme form of ethics upon my audience.

She thinks of Elizabeth Costello, the protagonist in J.M. Coetzee's eponymous novel, who travels the world giving lectures on the lives of nonhuman animals.

In the shower, she listens to a radio segment about food waste. Individuals waste approximately 4.4 pounds per day, the radio seg-ment states. As she pulls a soap scum-covered clump of hair out of the bathtub drain, she thinks, *I need to start composting.*

On a walk with Ian Hatcher, she explains how the novel never escapes the year 2020. It is three years later, and it is still 2020. "My protago-nist is going to start eating meat," she says.

"Maybe she should eat a chicken," Ian Hatcher says, referring to the end.

Dream-content: In a YouTube video, a chicken is in the center of Claire's room, pooling blood.

The meal starts off like countless others around the world, Claire says, kneeling alongside the chicken. *But then, dear reader*, Claire says, *Things take a different turn.*
    I can't wait to eat the brain, she says.
    The heirloom tomatoes gasp.
    With her hands covered in blood, Claire licks blood from bone.

One of the heirloom tomatoes cuts an eyeball in half.

One of the heirloom tomatoes is pink.

Claire dips her hand into a bowl of blood and tastes it.

The chicken's belly is opened; more blood is collected.

A man licks blood from a knife.

But this is not his story.

Claire takes the knife from his hand and slices his eyeball.

Claire wastes nothing; she uses every part of the animal, Ian Hatcher says in a text-to-speech voice.

In a text-to-speech voice, Simone Weil asks: *Is this any worse, really, than eating at Applebee's, comfortably far-removed from the business of the killing floor? Or is it, in fact, a more honest relationship with our dinner?*

Maybe she should eat a chicken, Ian Hatcher says, referring to the end.

Or maybe she should kill a fox instead, Simone says.

Dream-content: Our protagonist is wearing an all-white jumpsuit. She is standing in the center of a bright white room, holding a knife.

A fox enters. Its fur is orange; its eyes are yellow. One thinks of citrus, honeysuckle, the sun. It has a long nose and a pair of slender ears—the better to hear her with, or the better to hear the low voice with—and the end of its body is occupied by a tail.

Simone Weil: *The cross as a balance, a lever.* Its teeth—sharp in the front and flat in the back—serve to tear into anything it finds: birds, insects, earthworms, grasshoppers, beetles, blackberries, plums and mollusks and crayfish; amphibians and small reptiles; fawns and newborn lambs. A brood of chickens. A single hen.

It is plausible the fox does not know it is approaching the end. The walls in the room are tile and glossy. Red is the color of blood, apples, Santa Claus, and the Republican party. *Sensing what the subject can bear of anxiety puts you to the test at every moment*, a French psychoanalyst writes. But who is the subject: the dreamer or the creature? The fox or the hen? The conscious mind—the ego—or another entity external to the mind, which makes a sound that grants the mind pause in a moment of mercy?

She admires the knife she holds, how its metal reflects light in juxtaposition to her life's dark period, and imagines the horror of doing harm to the fox—stabbing it, gutting it, digging a grave for it, burying it. In her mind, she has murdered it so many times; all she wants to do now is be still, to sit alone and listen to a quiet room, and to the strangers in it, and to close her eyes and recite a prayer. *Fox in hell*, she would recite. *Hallowed fox*, she would recite. *Thy time has come.*

Grant me stillness and mercy, and help me to not kill thou who has trespassed against me. And lead neither of us into hell, but deliver us from ourselves, and toward our souls. Amen.

Following the recitation of this prayer, she is as fearful of the knife as she is reverent. She immediately runs the knife under water, hangs it over the stove on the magnetic strip where other knives reside. If she forgives, she is an apologist; if she doesn't, she is forever a hen. The tension between these ways of being in the world is directed both vertically and horizontally, and it remains unclear which direction to choose.

Alternatively, she pictures herself hunting under the cover of darkness, opening the fox's door, gaining entrance, then grabbing it in her mouth and tearing it apart like—

I cannot think it.

Nor can I dream it.

May he be happy, may he be loved, may he be free from suffering.

To which the fox rolls his eyes: *Who is your loving-kindness litany actually sparing?*

*
**

I dedicate my book to you. It occurs to me that this entire book is about you. I did not know this when I began writing it. Right away, however, I incorporated the images you gave me: a bed, a boat, a slaughtered chicken. A popcorn kernel. A bee. Sometimes, I think we communicate telepathically, as when we walked together in an institutional corridor and thought of the same song—"Cold, Cold Water"—or when we wrote the same sentence at parallel moments in different locations, or when you unburied the painting depicting a parent holding their child and we became the painting depicting a parent holding their child. Horizontally, it looked like a clown. Vertically, it represented two subjects mourning. And so we situated ourselves neither on an x or y axis, but around a table where we practiced contentment.

Before you, I did not know security. Security meaning the sort of love—romantic or non-romantic—that feels anchoring, consistent, close: a relationship in which neither person worries the other will pull away, leave them. I did not know what a "secure attachment" was until I read a self-help book, and I'm not sure I'll ever know another. At the table where we dined each night when we nightly dined, you told me I will meet someone who loves me, and they will have excellent taste not only in food, but also music.

This book is yours I am writing it for you take it. The chicken is the image we use to talk about the chicken; the fox is the image we use to talk about the fox. The fox came and slaughtered your parent's chicken, and you talked to me about it on the phone, and together we mourned it.

You need to eat, you said. Have you had dinner?

No, I have not eaten dinner. It's not that I'm depriving myself; it's that I am able to run on so very little. On so very little I am able to run, depleting myself all the time. You are having trouble eating, someone says, and someone else types something into the Internet—the great void—about deprivation being the problem of vegetarian cooking. When I say I am now eating chicken, a mutual friend says there is a communist journal with an entire issue devoted to constrained diets and eating disorders. I say I am writing a novella about Simone Weil and he says, yes, it is about her too.

Another friend says how funny it is I am eating chicken; chicken is what I eat too. I did not tell this friend about you, or about how we stood in the grocery store studying nutrition facts. You asked how many calories I had consumed that day and I said, I do not count them. Instead, I let my body run.

At Christmas, I tattooed upon my wrist an empty set: { }. To you, the empty set invoked an object in JavaScript, and so you say it's meaningful. The empty set to me is emblematic of love, or the couple form, or a parent and their child, or a caesura, or a breath, or austerity, or deprivation, or lack, or a bag filled with air: something containing nothing.

When we love, we give what we lack. I love you, and so I cooked you dinner. You brewed a pot of tea for me and bought me a bag of cookies that contain the good fat. I ate them while lying on your bed listening to "Fantastic Analysis," and as the guitars produce notes that float upwards toward the ceiling, I felt happy for the first time.

The concept of happiness weighs heavily on our spirits, Sara Ahmed writes, and I teach a chapter from her book The Promise of Happiness *about this idea. On the grass with my students (before the pandemic began), we discussed negative emotions. Why don't we ever frame so-called positive emotions as negative emotions, one student asked. For example, what happens if we consider happiness a negative emotion, or love, or joy? I am not sure how to answer this question, but I know that these two years have brought me closer to it, cooking alone in the apartment. The eerie confluence of birdsong entwined with a seemingly endless litany of ambulance sirens. Writing letters to you. Eating carrot* salad. Trying to finish a song, a poem, an illustration. A photograph taken in the park that preserves the guilt of lost time. And the shame of that guilt. Deprivation, fatality, bereavement.

Writing these pages, I felt gleeful anger, maniacal grief. I constrained my diet as a result of these feelings and called it loving-kindness. To some extent, it was. I said my piece. As I cooked, I prayed, and as I prayed, I imagined myself cooking next to a ghost. And because I practiced loving-kindness, I loved this ghost. I granted it patience. I became obsessed with it. I wondered: Is the ghost of a child inhabiting my apartment? At times, I wondered if the ghost was alive. Always I wondered if the ghost was me—my second body?

I want to only eat plants, but I don't want to eat only plants. I want to eat the flesh of everything; I want to be so close to something that I sink my teeth into its bones. And I want the act of writing to feel this way: like an excavation of each word—of each material letter-form—that leads me to a root. With my tongue licking its bones, I will ask: is the letter satiated?

I am not satiated; I am still hungry. The body needs fats, and carbohydrates, and protein, and butter. The body needs wings. The body is no longer slaughtered; now it is the yolk, which is the sun. It believes in rehabilitation mixed with reconciliation mixed with care mixed with anxiety mixed with skepticism mixed with retribution mixed with love. Thank you for your love, I want to say, and I feel self-conscious in my saying because I am an egg who has been unhatched for so long.

We are not free from suffering, but we are moving toward light. In an unexpected swerve away from the macabre, I am thinking now about moving toward light not only as an ethical responsibility to oneself, but to others, and to sustainable reserves of love and anger—which is to say, the world.

After you moved away, I missed eating dinner. I too will soon move away; I will live in a location more remote than the city, and I will think back on the period of time in which we ate dinner together *each night, and I will refer to this period of time as a model for security, and I will not take for granted the person I love—who has good taste in food and music; who is sad but loving; who believes language, like meat, contains bones. We will sit at a table, and I will call you. When I call you, I will say: Are you also eating? And you will say: I was thinking the same thing. I will say: What are you feeling? And you will say: A lot. I will say: How are you? And at the same time, you will say: How are you? To which I respond, looking out the window at the land, the sunset, the trees: I am not hopeful, but I am at peace.*

ACKNOWLEDGMENTS

Versions of stories in this book first appeared in the following publications: *A) Glimpse) Of), Black Sun Lit, The Brooklyn Rail, The Chicago Review, DIAGRAM, The Elephants, Fanzine, Fonograf, Forever,* and *Harp & Altar.* Thank you to all of the editors with whom I worked.

Gravity and Grace, The Chicken and the Egg, or: How to Cook Everything Vegetarian incorporates language from Simone Weil's *Gravity and Grace* (tr. Emma Crawford and Mario von der Ruhr), Clarice Lispector's "The Egg and the Chicken" (tr. Giovanni Pontiero), and M.F.K. Fisher's *How to Cook a Wolf,* among other sources listed in this book's Works Cited. The subtitle *How to Cook Everything Vegetarian* references the eponymous cookbook by Mark Bittman.

/

Thank you forever to Naomi Falk at Archway Editions, my editor.

Thank you to Daniel Power, Chris Molnar, Nicodemus Nicoludis, and Caitlin Forst at Archway Editions.

Thank you to Adrian Shirk, my longtime friend and literary agent.

Thank you to Jaclyn Gilbert, founder of Driftless Literary.

Thank you to my students and colleagues in the Writing Department at Pratt Institute, especially Beth Loffreda, Kath Barbadoro, aracelis girmay, and Alysia Slocum Laferriere.

Thank you to my teachers and cohort at Pulsion: The International

Institute of Psychoanalysis and Psychoanalytic Psychosomatics.

Thank you to Diego Zayas for the turtle illustration that accompanies "A Story About a Turtle Who Retreats Into Her Shell and Becomes a Real Girl."

Thank you to Anastasios Karnazes, Blake Butler, Ian Hatcher, Anna Moschovakis, Chris Allen, Jo Eidman, Brandon Wilner, Bryce Wilner, Caroline Carlsmith, Olivia Crough, Patrick Cottrell, Jeff Alessandrelli, Judd Morrissey, Cam Scott, Sav Hampton, Erica Ammann, Em Seely-Katz, Leia Bradley, Tracy Danes, Alec Niedenthal, Yashua Klos, Ross Gay, Ottessa Moshfegh, Jamie Stewart, Amalia Soto, Allie Rowbottom, Jamieson Webster, Amina Cain, Cléa Liquard, Lee Kuczewski, Cathryn Dwyre, Chris Perry, Anjali Khosla, Megan Boyle, Kristin Hayter, Laura Elrick, Diego Antoni, J †Johnson, Danniel Schoonebeek, Uche Nduka, Christopher Rey Pérez, Travis Holloway, Sarah Jean Grimm, Patty Gone, Emily Martin, Gregory S. Moss, Christian Hawkey, Timothy Terhaar, Gracie Leavitt, Willis Arnold, Carolyn Cale, Eric Roy, Sammy Maine, Jonnie Baker, Will Newman, John Cayley, Leigh Davis, Alexis Almeida, Kyra Simone, Anna Gurton-Wachter, Eduardo Zayas, Hokyu JL Aronson, Chelsea Hodson, Heather Christle, Mary Baumer, and Jim Baumer. These people—and many others who are not listed here—read and responded to versions of stories that appear in *Kind Mirrors, Ugly Ghosts*; blurbed *Kind Mirrors, Ugly Ghosts*; provided me with space and time to write; influenced these stories; and/or otherwise provided nourishment, support, friendship, care.

Thank you, Katie Eastburn, for your optimism and encouragement to advocate for myself and my art.

Thank you, Liz Bishop, for your good humor, and a quiet space to rest.

Thank you, Emily Schlesinger, for our work together, and for inspiring *Kind Mirrors, Ugly Ghosts*, by means of transference. This book is also yours.

Thank you, Nik Slackman, for believing in my writing and encouraging me to complete this book. *Kind Mirrors, Ugly Ghosts* would not exist without your resolute support, editorial guidance, friendship, love.

Thank you to my parents.

Thank you, Woebegone.

WORKS CITED

"Animal Rights Uncompromised: Catch-and-Release Fishing." PETA, www.peta.org/about-peta/why-peta/catch-and-release-fishing.

Aragon, Louis. "Suicide." 1926.

Avildsen, John G., director. Rocky. United Artists, 1976.

Baier, Sibylle. *Colour Green*. Orange Twin Records, 2006.

Baier, Sibylle. "I Lost Something in the Hills (Video)." YouTube, 8 Nov. 2014, www.youtube.com/watch?v=N-oERBst8Lo.

Balibar, Étienne. *Politics and the Other Scene*, trans. Jones et al. Verso, 2002.

Brown, Elizabeth Anne. "How Humans Are Messing Up Bee Sex." National Geographic, 11 Sept. 2018, www.nationalgeographic.com/animals/article/honey-bee-sex-mating-pesticides-humans-news.

Brown, Margaret Wise. *The Runaway Bunny*. Harper, 1942.

Carroll, Lewis. *Alice's Adventures in Wonderland and Through the Looking-Glass*. Penguin, 2003.

"Catch and Release Fishing." *National Park Service*, www.nps.gov/subjects/fishing/catch-and-release-fishing.htm.

Chytilová, Věra, director. *Daisies (Sedmikrásky)*. Ústřední Půjčovna Filmů and Kouzlo Films Společnost, 1966.

"*Daisies* - As Pequenas Margaridas - Comedy 1966 - Ivana Karbanová - Jitka Cerhová - Full Movie (Video)." YouTube, 1 Feb. 2022, www.youtube.com/watch?v=JEIfplmJoJ4.

Deparle, Jason. "111 Held in St. Patrick's AIDS Protest." *The New York Times*, December 11, 1989.

Fisher, M.F.K. *How to Cook a Wolf*. North Point Press, 1988.

Girl Ray. "Preacher." *Earl Grey*. Moshi Moshi, 2017.

Han, Byung-Chul. *The Burnout Society*. Stanford University Press, 2015.

Hanh, Thich Nhat. *How to Love*. Parallax Press, 2014.

Hecker, Tim. *Haunt Me, Haunt Me Do It Again*. Substractif, 2001.

Holzer, Jenny. *Truism: Expiring for Love is Beautiful but Stupid*. 1994.

Joy Division. *Unknown Pleasures*. Factory Records, 1979.

Ka-Tzetnik 135633. *House of Dolls*, trans. Moshe Kohn. Senate, 1997.

Kelley, Mike. *Educational Complex*. 1995, Whitney Museum of American Art, New York.

Kelly, Richard, director. *Donnie Darko*. Pandora Cinema and Newmarket Films, 2001.

Kipnis, Laura. *Against Love: A Polemic*. Vintage, 2004.

Korine, Harmony, director. *Gummo*. First Line Features, 1997.

Kruger, Barbara. *Untitled (Your Body Is a Battleground)*. 1989, The Broad, Los Angeles.

Leclaire, Serge. *Psychoanalyzing: On the Order of the Unconscious and the Practice of the Letter*. Stanford University Press, 1998.

Lispector, Clarice. "The Egg and the Chicken." *Selected Crônicas*, trans. Giovanni Pontiero. New Directions, 1996.

"Lonely Souls." *Twin Peaks*, created by David Lynch and Mark Frost, season 2, episode 7. Lynch/Frost Productions, 1990.

Ngai, Sianne. *Ugly Feelings*. Harvard University Press, 2007.

Preminger, Otto, director. *Bonjour Tristesse*. Columbia Pictures, 1958.

"Rainbow Sherbert." *Baskin-Robbins | Rainbow Sherbet*. www.baskinrobbins.com.sg/content/baskinrobbins/en/products/icecream/flavors/rainbowsherbet.html

Scalapino, Leslie. "From *Chameleon Series*." *boundary 2*, vol. 14, no. 1/2, 1985, pp. 27–29.

Sill, Judee. *Heart Food*. Asylum Records, 1973.

Smog. "River Guard." *Knock Knock*. Drag City, 1999.

Spacemen 3. "Set Me Free/I've Got the Key." *Recurring*. Fire Records, 1991.

The Sundays. "Can't Be Sure." *Reading, Writing, and Arithmetic*. DGC Records, 1990.

Super Mario World. Super Nintendo Entertainment System, 1991.

Suzuki, Shunryu. *Zen Mind, Beginner's Mind*. Shambhala, 2011.

"Thank You Shopping Bag." *International Plastics*, www.interplas.com/thank-you-bags/10-x-5-x-18-p-mb-t-18tk.

"Tropical Fish - Coral Predators" (screenshot). *Aquarium of the Pacific*, www.explore.org/livecams/aquarium-of-the-pacific/.

Twin Peaks, created by David Lynch and Mark Frost. Lynch/Frost Productions, 1990-91.

The Velvet Underground. "I'll Be Your Mirror." *The Velvet Underground & Nico*. Verve Records, 1967.

"Verne Troyer/Hines Ward." *Celebrity Wife Swap*, produced by Vince Anido et al, season 4, episode 2. Zodiak USA, 2015

Weil, Simone. *Gravity and Grace*, trans. Emma Crawford and Mario von der Ruhr. Routledge, 2002.

Wenders, Wim, director. *Wings of Desire* (*Der Himmel über Berlin*), 1987.

Woodman, Francesca. *Yet another leaden sky, Rome* (I.143.1), May 1977-August 1978. 1978. *Artnet*, www.artnet.com/artists/francesca-woodman/yet-another-leaden-sky-rome-i1431-may-1977-august-a-BNoKge85o-f2vtaByN2kQg2.

Woolf, Virginia. "Suicide Note." March 28, 1941. en.wikisource.org/wiki/Virginia_Woolf_suicide_note.

Other notes:

Bee sex images in *Gravity and Grace, The Chicken and the Egg, or: How to Cook Everything Vegetarian* via *Irish Examiner*, PBS, *The Scientist*, *Purdue University*, and *Quora*.

ASCII art in *Gravity and Grace, The Chicken and the Egg, or: How to Cook Everything Vegetarian* modified via ascii.co.uk.

Woebegone ASCII art created from an original 35mm photograph by Claire Donato converted to ASCII art using manytools.org/hacker-tools/convert-images-to-ascii-art.

The ASCII star field art throughout this book was inspired by Everest Pipkin's @tiny_star_field Twitter bot and assembled by Claire Donato.